THE DESPERADO
WHO STOLE BASEBALL

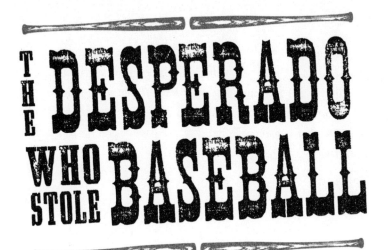

THE DESPERADO WHO STOLE BASEBALL

John H. Ritter

PHILOMEL BOOKS

IN ACKNOWLEDGMENT

I owe great thanks to Beth Brust and Stacey Goldblatt, my writing buds; Michael Green, my editor and story starter; Tamra Tuller, my editor's fail-safe and logician; Cheryl Ritter, my dream wife and visionary, too much to say. And Mrs. Ritter's fifth-grade class of 2008 at Explorer Elementary Charter School, feedbackers *brillantes*.

con mucho aloha,

J H R

PHILOMEL BOOKS

A division of Penguin Young Readers Group.
Published by The Penguin Group. Penguin Group (USA) Inc., 375 Hudson Street, New York, NY 10014, U.S.A. Penguin Group (Canada), 90 Eglinton Avenue East, Suite 700, Toronto, Ontario M4P 2Y3, Canada (a division of Pearson Penguin Canada Inc.). Penguin Books Ltd, 80 Strand, London WC2R 0RL, England. Penguin Ireland, 25 St. Stephen's Green, Dublin 2, Ireland (a division of Penguin Books Ltd). Penguin Group (Australia), 250 Camberwell Road, Camberwell, Victoria 3124, Australia (a division of Pearson Australia Group Pty Ltd). Penguin Books India Pvt Ltd, 11 Community Centre, Panchsheel Park, New Delhi - 110 017, India. Penguin Group (NZ), 67 Apollo Drive, Rosedale, North Shore 0632, New Zealand (a division of Pearson New Zealand Ltd). Penguin Books (South Africa) (Pty) Ltd, 24 Sturdee Avenue, Rosebank, Johannesburg 2196, South Africa. Penguin Books Ltd, Registered Offices: 80 Strand, London WC2R 0RL, England.

Text copyright © 2009 by John H. Ritter.
Map illustration copyright © 2009 by John S. Dykes Illustrations, Inc.

Published simultaneously in Canada. Printed in the United States of America.
Design by Richard Amari. Text set in Life Roman.

Library of Congress Cataloging-in-Publication Data
Ritter, John H., 1951– The desperado who stole baseball / John H. Ritter. p. cm. Summary: In 1881, the scrappy, rough-and-tumble baseball team in a California mining town enlists the help of a quick-witted twelve-year-old orphan and the notorious outlaw Billy the Kid to win a big game against the National League Champion Chicago White Stockings. Prequel to: The boy who saved baseball. [1. Baseball—History—Fiction. 2. Billy, the Kid—Fiction. 3. Orphans—Fiction. 4. Frontier and pioneer life—California—Fiction. 5. California—History—1850–1950—Fiction.] I. Title. PZ7.R5148De 2009 [Fic]—dc22 2008016901

ISBN 978-0-399-24664-7
1 3 5 7 9 10 8 6 4 2

This one is for my amazing uncle Mr. George Riser,

family man, coach, Senior Olympian,

American hero, full of grace.

With love, John

And to the memory of the courageous

Alfred E. "Fred" Coleman

gold miner, cattleman, former slave

who discovered gold in the Kwee-A-Mak Mountains,

starting the San Diego gold rush of 1869,

giving rise to Julian, California

He who hits 'em where they ain't
Three of ten is a player great.
Ah, but he who hits 'em where they ain't
Four times of ten becomes a saint.

—Cavestone etching
discovered in 1916

In the very big inning . . .

The gruff-and-tumble founders of Dillontown, California, were a scrappy bunch. From fistfighting misfits and cattle rustlers to gold-digging drunkards and cardsharp hustlers. And that's just the women.

The men were all that, plus they smelled bad.

However, over the years, that hardscrabble gold-mining camp began to attract a great big inning of a more civilized folk wishing to settle the boomtown down. And no matter from whence they came, from El Paso, Texas, to Bangor, Maine, they would each and all tell you that it was the Dillontown Nine Baseball Club, the likes of which America had never seen, that'd drawn them west. With fellows like Long John Dillon and Shadowfox Coe, Blackjack Buck and Fence Post Hayes, that rip-rollicking ball-walloping baseball team had built as high and as mighty a reputation as any club in all the land.

But one day, everything changed. Riding along that westward trail came some wild and cagey *hombres*, including none other than one William H. McCarty Antrim Bonney, erstwhile known as Billy the Kid—the cold-blooded killingest, back-stabbing stealingest, double-crossing, double-dealingest desperado on the sundown side of the Mississipp'. Or so folks say.

In Dillontown, we say something else.

May 5, 1881. Somewhere in the California desert . . .

The bullet ripped into the crown of the boy's hat with such force, it blew his black felt derby into a cactus patch. Startled, he hunched forward in the saddle, teeth-whistled into his horse's ear, and spurred that bronc with boots a-flying.

The next bullet nearly kissed his cheek. Gripping the baseball bat stowed in his rifle holster, he unstirruped a foot and swung himself to the safer side of the saddle.

"Hee-yaw!" he yelled, and he kept blasting whistle bursts until the galloping steed surrendered to its brighter instincts and bucked the boy off into a sandy wash, then streaked away.

The boy dropped, falling, cannonballing through sand and sage toward the tall canyon wall and into the thin shadowline of a small rock cave.

His sudden arrival did not set well with the silver-gray sidewinder coiled within, which had likely been resting in cool comfort until then. When that rattlesnake's rattlesnap began, the stark choice between being snakebit or leadball hit rose up quick in the boy's mind.

Figuring the shooter in those granite cliffs to be decidedly less accurate than an agitated, close-range snake, he darted back out of solid cover and dove under the branches of a mesquite bush in the middle of the river-wash canyon.

He'd been warned about Apaches, as well as thieves, but he had thus far avoided both, keeping to the whisper of less-traveled trails. It seemed to him, however, that neither of those parties would fire from afar, when a simple face-to-face ambush would've been more appropriate.

"Hey!" he shouted, hearing his voice echo off the tall valley walls. "I have no money."

Silence.

"I'm just a boy!" Again the lifeless cliffs stood quiet. High in the sky, three red-tailed hawks sailed in wide circles.

He searched northward, up into the crook of the rocky canyon, for a trace of his startled horse, but saw none, until he caught a tailflicker in the late afternoon light. It would take a daring sprint, but if he could reach the horse, he'd have a chance.

Hoping to pinpoint the shooter's location, he called again. "I'm no claim jumper. Is that what you think?"

Gaining no clue from that attempt, he grabbed a stone and flung it some thirty yards into the brush as a decoy. Hearing it hit, he then dashed the opposite way, toward his horse, as desperate and determined as if he were legging out a last-inning infield hit to keep the game alive.

Arriving safely in the shadow of the canyon wall past the first bend, he spotted his horse still up ahead in the open ravine, grazing on bunchgrass.

4

It would take one more sprint. Hugging the canyon wall, he crept slowly toward a dash-off point—until a small avalanche of rocks clattered down and landed directly in front of him in a dusty heap.

He jumped back just as a rifleman dropped from the mountain and onto the pile of stones.

"Hold it, jackrabbit!" he said, his knees bent, a rifle perched at his hip. "Don't try nothing you won't live long enough to regret."

The boy's hands rose in surrender, and he began to do what he did best. He talked. "I told you, sir, I have no money nor items of value."

The young rifleman, maybe twenty years old, with a smooth, boyish face, stared forcefully. "If I wanted your money, you'd be dead by now."

"You desire my horse then? Shall I retrieve him?" He took a step.

"Freeze." Through gritted teeth, he added, "I got a horse."

"Then why in the 'tire nation are you trying to kill me?"

"If I wanted you dead . . ." The rifleman held his weapon chest high and let the sight of its long barrel finish his thought. He brushed back his wild blond hair, which splayed out from under a high-domed drover's hat.

His eyes danced from the boy to the length of canyon beyond. "Son," he said, "I was just trying to attract your attention."

"Well, sir, you attracted it."

"Good. Now, why are you following me? And who else is with you?" His eyes once again swept the canyon sides.

"I am only with my horse, sir—the roan yonder." He motioned with his head. "Or, I was until he bucked up and shed me rather rudely. And if I'm following you, it is by pure coincidence, having to do with the fact that you and I, sir, are on the same trail and heading in the same direction."

"And where's that?"

"Well, westerly, mostly. I'm on my way to the gold hills of San Diego."

"This here's an old Kumeyaay trail, quite a ways off the settlers' road."

The boy nodded. "Reckoned it would be safer."

"Is that what you reckoned?" The gunman, now sounding a notch less tense, smiled slightly, his front teeth protruding over his bottom lip a bit like a squirrel's grin. "You know who I am?"

The boy shook his head, but the very question planted a wild-patch of worry in the fertile fields of his mind.

"Put your hands down."

The boy obliged, lowering his arms, slow as a landing crow.

"Heard you coming half a mile away," said the rifleman. Now his clear eyes, tinted a see-through blue, covered that half mile in a flash-glance before shooting back at the boy. "What's the hurry?"

"Well, it's almost dark, and I'd hoped to reach San Diego County by nightfall. Beyond that, I have been advised by those in a position to know that the quicker I cross Apache territory, the longer I might walk this earth."

"Those are sound words. But you're long past it now." He steel-eyed the young rider again. "How old are you?"

"Seventeen." Reading a flinch of disbelief on the rifleman's face, the boy added, "Nearly."

"Nearly?" The man angled forward with a narrowed scowl. "Fifteen, then."

The man leveled his rifle at the boy. "Wanna think that over?"

Being tall for his age, the boy was vexed by the man's disbelief, and he jerked his hands up high again. "Twelve full years, if you must know," he spat, angered at having to resort to facts. "Plus pretty near eight months."

The man lowered the rifle. "Well, now, son. The truth has set you free. Hands down. You running off from home?"

Sensing a gentleness in the gunman's spirit, the boy slowly began to lay out his story. "I don't have a home, sir. My folks're dead. Shot and killed outside Tombstone, Arizona, in a bloody gun battle."

The man narrowed his focus. "Sorry to hear that. What happened?"

"What happened was, they were outlaws, sir. Desperados. And on that day, their luck turned cold." The boy now spoke in a hush. "A posse of forty men hunted 'em down, right up to our doorstep, and killed 'em like dogs. But I will tell you, that's how it is, being an outlaw. It is not all glory and sunshine."

"You don't say."

"Well, I do. Yes, sir. That's why, once I shot my way out of town, figured I'd better head out to the hills of Californ' where my uncle John owns a couple thousand acres of land and five hundred head of cattle. Plus a *hacienda*—which is a mighty house." At that, the boy clamped his jawbones tight, lest he spool out more yarn than he had a notion to weave.

But the gunman did not challenge his tale. His eyes seemed to light up as he sent them over the boy's head, across the dusty *arroyo*. "Five hundred head, huh? Sounds like Uncle John's doing all right for himself."

"Yes, sir. All from being a prospector, which is how he struck it rich enough to build a whole town named after himself. Plus put together the finest baseball team in all the land. I aim to do some gold mining myself out there."

The man studied the boy a glint. "Would that explain the pickax handle I saw sticking up out of your rifle stow?"

The boy glanced off, deciding that any man who could spot his fine-turned piece of ashwood from a canyon top, then fire a perfect warning shot into his hat, must possess the eye of an eagle in flight.

"That, sir, is a baseball bat, as I am a skilled practitioner of the sport. If you'll allow me to retrieve my horse, Homer, I'll show you." Seeing an eyebrow twitch as permission, the boy started off. Glancing back, he said, "Fact is, I am soon to participate in the greatest baseball match ever held." He tapped his cloth vest. "I carry a newspaper clipping describing the competition. I can read it to you if you like."

"Just keep walking."

"Well, sir, I hope you'll allow me to retrieve my hat as well. Bought it brand new on the day I left Wichita."

"Wichita? Thought you came out of Tombstone."

The boy caught himself. "Last year, it was. That's right. We moved around quite a bit, in fact—before we turned outlaw and left civilization to scandalize the territories."

"Keep walking."

"But, truly," said the boy. Reaching inside his cotton vest, he pulled out a folded clipping. With a dramatic snap, he shook it open. Using his finger as a guide, he began to read.

We, the Baseball Club of the great and glorious gold-mining community of Dillontown, California, being undefeated, do hereby declare ourselves Champion Baseball Club of America, and, as such, we are willing to meet and contest with any other top professional club who says we ain't, bar none.

Thus, we hereby propose a Series of Seven Games against the top teams from the top seven Baseball Leagues in America. Any Ball Club which defeats the Dillontown Nine will receive *One Thousand Dollars* in gold.

In addition, we propose a Grand Finale to be held on Sunday, May 8, 1881, between the Dillontown Nine and the National League Champion Chicago White Stockings, should they have the courage to accept our challenge. Each side shall put up *Ten Thousand Dollars* in cash or gold, winner take all, as well as the undisputed title of *Champion Baseball Club of America*.

Signed, Captain Long John Dillon, Owner and Manager of the Dillontown Nine Baseball Club.

The boy glanced up. "That's my uncle, Mr. John Dillon. And he's putting up a solid gold bat and ball worth ten thousand dollars. How do you like that? And I'm heading out to help his boys win that title." He folded the paper and put it away, feeling satisfied he had established the merit of his journey. However, the man's reaction was hard to read. Reaching for the reins of his red gelding, the boy also reached for camaraderie. "Have you ever played the grand game of baseball, sir?"

"Upon occasion."

Feeling relief at the man's answer, as well as a hint of brotherhood, the boy pulled Homer close and extended his hand. "My name is John Jefferson Jackson Dillon. Most folks call me Jack."

The man reached out slowly. They shook. "Henry," he stated in a gruff voice. "You handle a gun, Jack? Being an outlaw and all."

Sensing a tone of mockery, Jack released his grip. He now wished he actually owned a gun. "I can manage." Dissatisfied with how that sounded, he added, "I'll say this. You wouldn't want to test me." Instantly, he regretted that remark as well.

Henry didn't flinch, but continued moving his eyes past the boy, from side to side, never resting, always on the prowl. "Well, then," he said, "since you're headed where I'm headed, I say we trail up together."

Jack pondered the plus and minus of the bargain—riding with an eagle-eyed rifleman, albeit one who had almost killed him, versus riding as he had, being his own boss, free to pick his course, albeit being unarmed and alone in unknown territory and spending endless hours addressing the top of his horse's head for social comfort.

"Well, I don't know."

The man glared at him. "I wasn't giving you a choice."

Jack's heart boomed. He spoke slowly. "Oh, well then. Since you're not giving me a choice, all right, I guess." As a final stab at saving face, Jack added, "Long's you don't slow me down."

Henry grunted as he walked toward his own horse, deposited nearby in a dry creek mouth.

Jack hustled to catch up. "I aim to *earn* myself a top position on Uncle John's team, by the way, not get one handed to me based on kinship, if that's what you think. No, sir. Being a supreme caliber of player, fleet of foot, quick of hand, and rather clever, I aim to earn it, although I must say, a certain degree of humbleness disallows me from being any more specific than that."

He coughed into his hand, mounted his horse, took in a deep breath, then awaited Henry's response.

Henry held silent.

Jack Dillon was dispartial to silence. He favored noise and woo-haw. He favored action. But, as he followed the man toward his horse, all he could think to do was stand in his stirrups and try to spy that hat-snatching cactus patch so he could retrieve his hat.

Henry mounted his blue-steel dun, and in the church-hall silence that followed, both riders headed off for Jack's high-crowned derby.

Finally, Henry spoke. "Son, I'm going to give you one chance to back up and state your story all over again. From the beginning. But this time, tell me the version of which your mother would approve. Or I may just go and take your horse and leave you right out here to the buzzards and the outlaw gangs. ¿Comprende?"

"Yes, sir."

Jack's hat came into view now, resting on a cactus pad a bit downslope. He stopped his horse, dismounted, and fetched his black felt derby. Holding it aloft, he could see a flash of the daytime moon—a few parts shy of being full—right through the bullet holes, high in the eastern sky. He felt grateful for the heavenly sign, knowing, as all prodigious baseball players did, that a baseball moon was coming, and that good things always happened under a baseball moon.

Donning the hat, he whistled softly and remounted Homer.

"Henry," he began, as slowly as a crafty pitcher beginning his warm-ups with lob balls, "I admit—yes, sir—that due to my precarious predicament, I may have somewhat safeguarded a portion of the truth."

Henry gave a hint of a nod. "May have."

"Uh, yes. So let me just say that I'm on this road you've found me on because a long time ago I began to dream about the future. And right now, I'm out to pursue the three biggest dreams in my life."

Henry grunted again. "And those are?"

Jack cleared his throat. "Well, first, I have dreamed for quite a while of traveling to Californ' and striking it rich, favoring, as I do, the luxury, ease, and convenience of a wealthy life, albeit I've never known one."

Henry said nothing as both riders kept moving.

"Then one day," Jack continued, "my, uh—well, I received a letter." He coughed into his fist. "Yes. From my uncle, it was. Telling me all about his glorious baseball team. So that led to my second dream, which is to become a professional baseballist and play for my uncle's team, for I do happen to possess a measure of skill in this arena, as I may have mentioned."

Henry harrumphed.

Jack went on. "Anyhow, what I figured was, if I came out West, I could shoot two birds with one shot. Baseball *and* gold. So, about six weeks back, I joined a wagon train out of Kansas City that was headed for the Oregon Trail. I hired on as a cook's helper. But once we crossed the Rocky Mountains, the trail started snaking north. So I borrowed me a horse—"

"Borrowed?"

Jack whipped off his holey hat and whacked his knee with it. "You are the confounded detail-mindedest man I ever met. Now, I'm doing my best here." He blew out a breath. "All right, I *took* one—a very lonely looking horse, I might add, one that I judged to be in dire need of socialization, tethered as he was to the very last wagon in the train."

"You being a social sort and all."

"Yessir, yessir. Anyhow, the journey has taken me longer than

I'd supposed, but now I'm crossing the deserts of Californ', and I'm getting close. Rounding third and heading to the home stone, you might say."

Henry spurred his horse into a trot. "So what's dream three?"

Jack nudged Homer forward to keep pace. "Well, that's the one I'm pretty sure will never come true," he said, looking out into the distance. "I wish one day to ride the Wild West with the world-famous outlaw Billy the Kid."

Henry whipped his head sideways, slowed his horse, and gave Jack a hard squint. "Hold it right there. Now, why would you ever want to ride with the likes of that no-good, man-killin', cattle-rustlin' son of a sidewinder?"

The reaction startled Jack. "Doggone, Henry, where I come from, that's every boy's dream. Why, Billy the Kid is the wiliest gunfighter, the fastest draw, the sharpest shooter in the world. He can even shoot a silver dollar out of the sky."

"Where'd you get all that malarkey?"

"Oh my gosh, Henry. Don't you pay attention? All that—all that is common knowledge. From here to New York City."

"Is that a fact?"

"Yessir. And I believe I could be a big help to an outlaw like him."

"A big help? How would you be any kinda help to that ornery cuss?"

"I could be his scout, for one thing." This was one of Jack's more recent ideas, but as soon as he said it, he liked it even better.

"His scout?"

"Sure. I could ride off and spy out the situation up ahead. And then I'd communicate with him using secret signs. No one would suspect a boy, see? I have good eyes, too. As good as you."

"Oh, you do, do you?" For some reason, Henry seemed to take that as a challenge. He rose up in his stirrups, staring off toward the horizon. "Okay, see that roadrunner in the clearing up ahead, between those two small boulders?"

Jack peered into the dusk. He thought he saw something. "Sure, I do. My old grandpa could see that."

"What's he got in his mouth?"

Jack stared harder into the dusk. He now realized he saw no roadrunner—he barely saw the two rocks. So he did what he did best. "Do you mean that roadrunner there with the lizard in his beak? Or the one yonder swallowing the snake?"

Henry sat back in his saddle and said nothing for the longest time, staring, squinting. Finally, he tipped back his hat and said, "You, son, have an imagination that knows no fear."

Jack felt the heat rise inside of him at having been caught so easily in a falsehood once again. This fellow was far harder to fool than he'd first thought.

Suddenly a panic swept through Jack. Why *did* Henry make him ride along? What was he planning to do with him? Could Homer outrun Henry's sleek horse? Could Jack slip away later in the dead of night?

Then it struck him like a beanball to the noggin. Henry was a lawman! Of course! He was a lawman, hot on the trail of a dozen desperados who roamed the Wild West, just like in all the dime novels he'd been reading. And of course that was why he'd been seeking the truth.

"You're a man of the law, aren't you, Henry? That's why you're taking me with you, ain't it?" A wave of excitement passed through him. "Do you think I'm Billy the Kid?" Jack slapped his thigh in realization, growing serious as he thought about it. "Dang, I was afraid that might happen. Me being a desperado and a kid and whatnot."

Twisting his mouth into a crooked grimace, Henry glared at him, saying, "I was a lawman, son. But I no longer carry a badge."

"Oh, so you're a bounty hunter. You're out to collect all the rewards on all the heads of all the outlaws in the West, aren't you?" Jack glanced off toward the dark purple mountains that loomed over the iron-red rockscape ahead, to consider the notion. "If this don't beat all. Admit it, Henry. You thought I was Billy the Kid. That's why you rounded me up. I *knew* it could happen, since people don't really know what that outlaw looks like."

And for that very reason, the next bullet, one that split the gray light between the two riders like a lightning shaft, should not have surprised Jack much at all.

3

It was every man for himself. As more shots splintered the sky, Jack and Henry galloped across the rocky ocotillo-dotted desert as fast as their mounts could flee.

Ambushed! thought Jack. By outlaws. I was right about Henry being a lawman—dead right!

He aimed for a low, distant bluff that sat straight ahead of him like an island in the middle of the flat land while Henry rode off toward a sister bluff a hundred yards south. Just keep riding, pardner, Jack told himself. Ride like you're heading for home and the shortstop has the ball.

"Hee-yaw!" he cried, and teeth-whistled rapid bursts.

More shots split the evening air as Jack reached the stony outcrop ahead, only to see that it was not tall enough to give him shelter for long. Riding past, he glanced back to try to spot the shooter. A lone horseman rode through the sandy wash he and Henry had just left. Jack spied Henry turning and disappearing into a finger canyon to his left, so Jack whistled again and rode off into the sundown, seeking another streambed or ravine to duck into. Two more shots whizzed by just above his head.

The shooter, it seemed, had given up on Henry and was pursuing Jack.

Up ahead he noticed a stand of cottonwood trees. Temporary shelter again, he decided, unless he could somehow ditch Homer and hide out on foot. The horse was spooked, no doubt. He would run forever if Jack could just dismount in a hurry—onto a soft spot.

No such luck. All he could see as he passed the trees was more rock-hard desert. But not jumping would be worse. So he risked it. Deciding the trees had momentarily blocked him from view, Jack leapt from the saddle, landing boots first, then tumbled onto the desert floor, just missing a knee-high boulder but getting scuffed by several cracked cobbles scattered beyond.

On forearms and knees, he lizard-crawled back toward the biggest tree, wincing at the streak of pain he felt run along the side of his hand. Rising and gripping a tall branch, he began to climb.

The horseman approached, whipping his mount to gain speed.

The tree was too sparse of leaves to hide Jack completely, but he leaned into it, hoping to blend in and become part of the trunk to a joggle-eyed observer.

It was perfect. The man in all black rode past at full steam, his silver spurs jingling with the horse's bounding strides. Jack kept watching. Knowing he had once outdashed a young mare in a short burst, he figured that as soon as the horseman disappeared, he'd drop down and sprint toward the closest hill and up some rocky path too rugged for a horse to climb.

Problem was, the shooter never disappeared. In fact, he slowed to a halt.

It was only natural, Jack supposed, since Homer had not gone more than a hundred yards before he stopped at a downstream pool to slurp a little water.

The rider began to eyeball the tree.

Run for it, Jack told himself. Just run. Maybe the dusk will fog his eyes.

He dropped to the ground and lit off toward the nearest patch of boulders. Not good enough! The horseman wheeled around and galloped toward him. Ducking again, Jack scanned the dry riverbank he'd just ridden past for its steepest incline and saw one to the south, about a quarter mile away.

He ran for it, digging into the earth with all the strength his legs could offer. If he were cornered, would the man shoot him or try to ride up and capture him?

His answer came faster than his next thought—delivered by gunshot. He heard the bullets whistle by, but as long as he didn't feel them, he would keep on running.

Then Jack realized something. He was running *toward* the bullets. That is, they were not coming from behind. They were flying over his head from the very riverbank he was running for.

Henry! He must've followed his finger canyon alongside Jack, then scaled one side to see if he could head off the shooter.

And just like that, the hunter became the hunted. The horseman turned wide, circling back, and scrambled east, right past the trees, galloping back from whence he came as fast as he could ride.

Jack stayed where he was. Within minutes, Henry reappeared, on foot.

"That was pure genius," said Henry as he led his horse down from the small ridge above, laughing and talking to Jack as if they'd just happened to meet up at a barn dance one night. "It's one thing to be able to think on your feet. But I love to see thinking like that in the heat of a battle."

Whoa, now, thought Jack. Henry thinks I masterminded that little episode—getting the shooter to stop and turn so Henry could secretly pass him, setting up our *own* ambush. This was not exactly the case.

However, not being one inclined to dissuade another from holding a higher opinion of himself than he deserved, Jack simply nodded.

Then, tugging on his hat, he said, "Well, someone has to do the thinking around here. I just hoped you could see what I had in mind and lend a hand. But you did all right, son. You did all right."

Henry grinned as he swung into his saddle. "Let's go get your bronc, tree boy. When I said 'genius,' I was talking about your horse."

"Oh." Jack looked around. It was true. Homer had done more thinking than Jack had. Why run past water in country like this? Starting off after him, Jack said, "I knew that. What I just said there, Henry? That was a josh. I was simply attempting to add a small amount of humor to a tense situation."

"Well, you did do that," Henry said. "Smallest amount I've heard in a long time."

Jack paid him no mind as he trotted alongside. He had much more to discuss. "So who was that guy, Henry? Why was he shooting at us? And where do you think he went?"

"If we're lucky, he's riding on back to Yuma."

"Was he an outlaw? Was he Billy the Kid? Or Jesse James? Did he know you were once a famous lawman?"

Henry shook his head. "Never got the chance to ask." He continued riding, glancing behind from time to time but offering no more clues.

"Well, there's got to be some reason," Jack prodded. "Was he fixing to rob us?"

Henry said no more about it. They gathered Jack's horse and hit the trail once again, with Henry maintaining a grim silence.

As they rode along ancient sandy-graveled river bottoms under the gloamy light of the ever-brightening moon, the uncomfortable silence grew too much for Jack. He risked the lawman's anger one last time.

"Look, Henry. You haven't hardly told me a single thing about yourself. And I think I got a right to know."

Jack's demand was met with stony silence, which only worried him more.

"Doggone, Henry. You said you favored the truth. Well, I say holding back is the same as lying. Come on, now, say something."

Not much farther down the trail, Henry did just that. In a firm, matter-of-fact voice, he addressed the mountains ahead. "Listen up, Jack Dillon, and listen good. This is something you need to know from here on out."

Henry glanced back one more time, his eyes shifting from one stretch of the horizon to the other, then resettled. "There is a reason I brought you along with me. And it has nothing to do with me being a lawman. Or a bounty hunter. Because I ain't neither one."

As if a cold evening wind had just blown in, Jack felt a shudder ride through him.

"Twenty-one years ago," Henry continued, "I was born in New York City. In my lifetime, I've carried several names. Will McCarty, Henry Antrim. Sometime later, Billy Bonney. But nowadays, most folks refer to me as Billy the Kid."

Jack stared long and hard at the slight young man riding next to him. *Billy the Kid?* This baby-faced, blond-haired, blue-eyed lucky shot? Billy the Kidder was more like it. He blasted out a sharp laugh.

"All right," he said. "All right, Henry. You got me. Look, I promise I'll rope my stories in from now on. Lesson learned. Yes, you're right. I may still have stretched a point here or there. But aren't you the man who said the truth will set you free? That's all I was askin' for. The truth."

Henry looked deep into Jack's eyes. "Son, your story stretching don't bother me. Because I know I can get the truth out of you when I need to. But what I just told you was no story." He spurred his horse and jaunted ahead.

Jack felt a tenseness that caused his thoughts to cyclone up inside as he realized there was no way to disprove what Henry had just said. After all, there were no "wanted" posters. No photographs. Like most people, Jack only *assumed* he knew what Billy the Kid looked like. He had to be a bear of a man, Jack figured, riding tall in the saddle, to have become such a feared and dangerous outlaw. But then again, he wasn't precisely sure.

"Hold on," he called, studying the small, stoic figure ahead of him, the suspicious loner. "Henry, wait a minute." He rode forward. "Is that the truth? What you just said?"

"Truth."

"Because you believe in the truth."

Henry nodded. "In spots like this, son, it's only fair."

Jack could hardly ride. Gripping his saddle horn, he sputtered out, "You're B-B-Billy the Kid? You—you just shot your way out of prison? Hightailed it out of Lincoln County in a flurry of gunfire?"

He spurred Homer forward twenty feet in a burst of speed, only to stop and slide in the dirt, spinning the steed in a circle while waving his hat. "Hew-ta!" He rode back toward the notorious outlaw. "I just knew you were somebody convolutionary!"

As Jack passed by, Henry—now Billy—swatted at him with his own hat. "Hey! Stop that. Keep it down." Anger rose up in his voice. "If I wanted this whole countryside to know, I'd of sent out telegrams."

Jack halted a few strides away, but his mind was already so full of ideas, he could barely listen. All that planning for a day he thought would never come was about to pay off!

"How's this?" he offered. "From now on your name is Henry Dillon. All right? You'll be my older brother. Two baseball brothers is who we are. That way, no one would suspect it's you."

Billy tilted back, then dumped his head in disgust. "Brothers? Me, with blond hair, light skin, and you, black hair and dark as tanned leather? I don't think folks'd buy that."

"Ah, folks wouldn't know."

"You don't think your uncle might reason it out?"

"Oh." Doggone, thought Jack, what an all-seeing, think-of-everything outlaw he is. I am the luckiest boy on earth. "Well, that's true. He might."

"Look, it's bad enough me having to escort an unarmed boy. I don't need you pulling any of your half-wit shenanigans. You do offer me a bit of cover, though. No one would expect me to come riding in with a boy. So that puts you about one notch above being good for nothing." He paused as if to let that notion sink in before adding, "When we get there, all I really wanna do"—he shook his finger—"is lay low a while." He held up an open palm toward Jack, signaling him to calm down. "And sort things out. ¿Comprende, chivo?"

"Oh, don't worry about that." Jack's mind was whirling. "Me, I can lay low with the best of 'em. I can be a crawling king snake, if I want to. And I'm good with secrets. Shoot, you won't get a secret out of me. I'd rather tell a lie any day than circulate the official truth. You ought to know that by now."

"That I do, son. Fact, I like how you can dream up a tall tale on the spot. One reason I asked you along."

Jack caught himself not breathing and took in a huge breath. "It is?"

As they rode off, side by side, he took a moment to adjust to the idea that even though Billy may not have bought everything he'd tried to sell, the man still appreciated his merchandise. Fine with me, thought Jack. I am the sidekick of Billy the Kid. My wildest dream of all has come true first!

Every single thing Jack had done had been meant to bring

him to this point, he was sure, even if he'd had no idea what he was doing or why: leaving his small town outside St. Louis after the water illness took his parents and little brother, hopping the wagon train to head west, taking the horse for the trek into California. Inside, a sense of purpose had been building over the last few months. Now it all made sense.

And now he understood why this lone horseman had been so concerned about being followed and why he needed a sidekick to help him keep his shadow low. Every boy in Missouri, in New Mexico—in the land—knew about Billy the Kid. That he was a wild and desperate outlaw who'd been sentenced to hang and had just escaped from jail. That he had stolen cattle, horses, and money, and had taken the lives of many. That there was a reward on his head a mile high. *Two thousand dollars.* Five years' wages for most men.

And that Billy was wanted dead or alive.

Two weeks earlier, in the canyons of downtown Chicago . . .

They won't go," said Vernon Toots. The pale, round man narrowed his beady eyes so small, he looked for all the world like a factory rat. "They're a spoilt bunch of men, and your pretty boy, King Kelly, he's the worst."

William Hulbert, wealthy coal baron and owner of the Chicago White Stockings, sucked long and hard on his Cuban cigar, until the end glowed bloodred. From his elegant leather chair, he eyed Toots, his right-hand man, pacing in front of the boss's desk. "Now, let me tell you something, Tootsie." He aimed his cigar at the plump man's egg of a face, barking out each word with a cloud of smoke. "I'll get 'em to go. And A. G. Spalding will see to it. Or they'll never play baseball in this league again."

Toots scowled and turned, snugging his thumbs in the coin pockets of his leprechaun-green vest. He turned slowly in front of Hulbert's long mahogany desk, the centerpiece of this cold, damp office on the thirteenth floor of the Chicago Bank and Mercantile Building.

"You think you and Spalding," asked Toots, "are going to get baseball professionals earning one, two, three thousand dollars a season to ride a stagecoach into the devil's land just to play a band of goldfield cowboys?" He stepped to the silver spittoon planted at the base of the glass-topped ticker-tape machine and spat. "Bah," he said. "I can't see one speck of good coming out of all this."

"Ten thousand dollars in gold?" said Hulbert. "*And* a gold mine to boot. That's not good enough?"

"Who believes that? I sure don't. I think it's all bluff. This character, Dillon, has never shown anyone the gold. He's nothing but a washed-up ballplayer from Chickenswitch, Iowa, who's pieced together a ball club that picks off one squad of circus clowns after another. First, they build themselves a great reputation that no one can verify. Then he announces this ridiculous challenge, and we're supposed to jump? No one even knows if the club can pay up or whether that gold mine is worth a fiddler's dram."

"You'll know," said Hulbert, rising from his overstuffed chair to shuffle through a pile of newspapers at the edge of his massive desk.

"*I* will? How so?"

"Because I'm sending you out there early to snoop around." He yanked out a section of newspaper and shook it open. "And as far as jumping goes, listen to this. *Chicago Daily Tribune.* 'Will William Hulbert take up the gauntlet thrown down by John Dillon, the thirty-nine-year-old gold miner from Jefferson County, Missouri, and his upstart team? Or will Mr. Hulbert continue to play it safe, choosing to face only handpicked rivals from the so-called National League, the very league the coal baron created several years ago for his own amusement and vainglory?'" Hulbert flung the paper across the room into an oil painting depicting him standing stern-faced in front of an enormous mountain of coal. "Why, I ought to jump down that editor's throat with both feet! Not a word of truth!"

The paper flopped to the waxed-wood floor. Then the glass-domed ticker machine came alive atop its wooden pedestal. It began spewing out stock quotes, tick by tick, as the paper ribbon cascaded onto the floor. Hulbert hurried over to gather up the white paper tape and ripped off a piece several feet long. As the big man perused the cryptic messages, he kept right on talking.

"So you'll head on down to Dillontown, Toots, and find out all the scuttlebutt you can. Tell me first off how much that mine is worth. That gold bat and ball may be chicken feed next to the gold nuggets still left in that mine."

"I thought Spalding told us that mine was shut down."

"It is. But not for lack of gold, my man. For lack of heart." He ripped off another strip of tape. "From what I've heard since, Dillon doesn't have the heart to blast open his precious mountain and do what needs to be done to extract the rest of the gold that's buried inside."

He crumpled the ticker tape in his pink manicured hands, tossing the ball aside while striding toward the office door. He leaned through the doorway and called, "Miss Steinkalt! Sell Atchison, Topeka. And buy a thousand shares of Pacific Railroad. Pronto!" Without missing a beat, he turned back to Toots.

"Then I want you to file a report as to what sort of ballplayers they'll be putting on the field. I'll rely on your word, Tootsie. If all looks good, I guarantee I'll get these prima donnas down to Dillontown, including Cap Anson, George Gore, and King Kelly himself."

The man with the eyes of a rat frowned, asking solemnly, "When should I leave?"

"Tomorrow. You'll go by train, then by stage. Wire me your first report next week. By then I should be in Frisco with the ball club. They'll be wrapping up their Far West exhibition trip. If you like what you see, we'll head south and jump a steamer in Los Angeles to the San Diego port. From there, it's a two-hour coach ride to Dillontown. We can do the whole trip in two days and nights. That ten thousand dollars will just about meet my payroll for the whole 1881 season. So I'll be counting on it. But that old panned-out, played-out gold mine—that's the real prize. To the right man, that may be worth a queen's ransom."

"And if I don't like the looks of things? Say, for example, they really do have a crackerjack team?"

Miss Steinkalt entered with a stack of papers to sign.

Hulbert crushed his cigar into a silver ashtray, ignoring her. "In that case, you do what you need to do, Tootsie, to—shall we say—make things look better."

Leaning over to dip his pen into the inkwell, Hulbert's eyes filled with the smoke of smoldering ash. "I've never let a coal miners' union get the best of me, and I sure as hallelujah won't be letting a bunch of skunk-drunk, baseball-playing gold miners show me up. Do whatever is necessary to guarantee victory. Do you understand?" He signed a flurry of papers, and Miss Steinkalt hurried out.

Toots watched her leave, then resumed his pacing back and forth. "I wish you wouldn't call me Tootsie in front of her."

"Bah! You're too sensitive."

The rat-eyed man sent Hulbert a piercing look. Then, taking a deep breath and seeming to calm himself, he spoke in an even tone. "What if doing whatever is necessary should take extreme measures?"

"You're my vice president, aren't you?"

Toots stepped toward the window and did not bother answering.

Hulbert checked his wool vest pocket for his silver lighter and opened his box of cigars. "Then use a little vice. We're in an extreme business, my man."

Toots spun around and sneered out his reply. "Professional baseball? Compared to coal mining, it's child's play. I hardly call it extreme."

"The business of baseball, no, it's not extreme. Coal mining, no, as well." Hulbert snapped the flintstone twice, and the lighter wick glowed. "But that's not what I'm talking about. The business we're in is the business of making money—to the extreme." He drew in the flame.

Vernon Toots rubbed his puffy white hands together and grinned hard—so hard his beady eyes disappeared into the surrounding folds of flesh. Apparently, he was warming up to the idea.

Under the cloak of nightfall they rode.

Jack Dillon and Billy Bonney, the man who would now be introduced as "Bill Henry," worked their horses toward the sky-wide expanse of California mountains, looming ahead like rain-black thunderclouds beneath the brims of their hats. Urging their mounts with shushes, clicks, and pats, they finally began to ascend out of the dead-ocean sand of the desert floor.

"Countryside's changing," said Billy, lifting his chin toward the boulder-strewn foothills of scrub and mesquite at the base of the Kwee-A-Mak mountain range.

Using the helpful light of a nearly full moon he perused the trailways behind, finally telling Jack that he now felt sure they were no longer being followed by the shooter—or by anyone else.

"We'll hunt out a box canyon," said Billy, "in those little ridges up ahead and make camp for the night."

"Sounds good." Jack would now admit to feeling somewhat beat after his twelve hours of riding that day.

A while later, Billy picked the campsite, well hidden from the trail. It was set inside a long narrow canyon that butted up against a steep ridge, forming a wall at that end, "boxing" the riders and their horses in—and boxing trouble out.

Jack knew all about box canyons, but he did not know how Billy could have spotted one from so far away.

"Little things like that," said Billy, "you pick up on the trail. Reading the land, I call it."

He stooped at the waist, then knelt, and began gathering twigs near his feet. Jack followed his lead. Billy built a dense teepee-like stack with the twigs.

"In these parts," Billy added, "most canyons run east and west. Rarely does a canyon run north-south."

"Is that so?"

Jack dumped his sticks, then pulled a small box of matches from the front pocket of his jeans. Finding just three matchsticks left, he squatted next to Billy and lit the kindling wood using only one of them.

"Yes, it is." Billy leaned closer and softly blew into the flame.

Once it looked like the fire would catch, Billy rose and broke off a few thicker pieces of brush, snapping them with his boot heel.

"So if you ever lose your bearings," Billy continued, "get up on a knoll and look around. You can read the direction you're heading in just by seeing which way the canyons run."

"Well, doggone!" Jack leaned back, watching the flames flicker and jump from branch to branch. "Wonder why that is."

"Well, like I say, look around." Billy used a branch to point toward the box end of the canyon. "Most mountain ridges, like the one we're facing, run north-south. So when the rain runs off their backs, it flows to the east or to the west, and eventually, that's what builds the canyons. And a box canyon, that's just one that has a steeper ridge at the head of it. Cattle rustlers like 'em because they keep their stock safe and out of sight."

"I never knew any of that," said Jack. "And here I've been on the trail for all this time."

Billy humphed, feeding more branches to the fire. He then walked to his supplies and broke out some jerky strips and a can of beans.

"Last one," he said.

Using a hunting knife, he opened the can but kept the lid on, angled up. He then set the tin can right in the fire. They watched it cook for a while.

"What do you plan to do once we get there, Billy? In Dillontown."

"As I say, lay low. Have a look around."

"Look around for what?"

"Well, let's see." He stretched back as he spoke. "Gonna have to find me a good poker game before too long. Running low on funds."

"A poker game? Don't you worry about folks recognizing you?"

"Lots of folks recognize me." He pointed east. "But they're all back there now."

Jack kept silent a moment, thinking. "But there's that big reward. Suppose—"

"Suppose you just eat your meat and let me take care of me." He used two sticks as blacksmith tongs to lift the beans.

"Besides, a man would have to haul me clear back to Santa Fe, New Mexico, either on my horse or across it, to earn that reward. Sounds like a lot of bother, don't it?"

It did, thought Jack. But that didn't mean no one would try.

Billy stuck his knife into the smoky can of beans and stirred.

"But what I mean is, Billy, what about you and me? Are we just going to split up and go our separate ways?"

Billy arched his brow. "Now, did I say that? Why don't you just relax, and we'll see how things go."

"Okay by me," said Jack, feeling a grin roll across his face.

As they ate their meal of jerky and beans, Billy informed Jack that they would sleep just a few hours, until the wee morning, then begin their journey up the eastern, or desert, side of the range well before dawn.

"Long's we get an early start," said Jack. "Missed out on four or five days of baseball already."

Again, for a long while, neither of them spoke. Jack was content with chewing slowly while tumbling around in his mind the dream of actually seeing Dillontown tomorrow. Leaning back, he caught the glint of a red-tailed hawk's white breast as it landed behind a tall stand of boulders just up the ridge. In sunlight that would've been an ordinary sight. But to spot a day-hunter near midnight—Jack knew this sighting was pure good luck.

Billy finished up, scraping his tin plate with his knife. "I'd like to know something, son. What is it that's so attractive about baseball that you'd engage in a fifteen-hundred-mile trail ride just to get a chance to play?"

Jack peered down into the now-cool can of beans to scoop

out a few finely burnt specimens stuck to the bottom. He could tell Billy about the lucky coincidence of finding the name of his dad's long-lost brother in a St. Louis newspaper story. Or how his father had taught him all the finer points of baseball from the time he'd learned to walk. Or he could select his most recent concoctionary account, which, of the three, now appeared most appealing.

"Well, shoot, Bill Henry. I practically invented baseball."

Billy puffed out a laugh. "Oh, you did, huh?"

"Now, what's so funny about that? Somebody had to invent it. Why not a ferocious desperado like me?"

"Well, because you're only twelve," said Billy, "and the game's been around for fifty years or more."

"Well, now, all right, all right. You got a point. Did I say invent? No, what I meant to say was '*re*-invent.' I aim to introduce a type of baseball that's never been seen before."

"How you figure on doing that?"

"Well, nice of you to ask. You see, it appears to some folks that over the last several years baseball has lost its spark. People have been losing interest because the game has gone slow and turned citified. But I have dreamed up new ways of playing, which I am very anxious to show to Uncle John."

"To spark up the game."

"Yes, sir. That's why I'm going. See, my pa was Uncle John's younger brother, but he lost touch with him years ago once he ran off to the goldfields and all. Mama used to say that"— Jack searched the sky a moment—"that Uncle John was the black sheep of the family. Yep. But he was a great baseballist, same as me, and I just know he'll appreciate all the ideas I've cooked up about fixing this game and turning it around."

Billy pushed himself to his feet and strode toward his bedroll, set closer to where the horses were tethered.

Jack followed, unrolling his shank of canvas next to Billy's. "But I do, Bill Henry. I have ideas that I know will advance the sport. And that's what's so attractive to me about baseball. I aim to fire up this game well into the future! Clear through the 1880s and beyond."

Jack bent forward, his hands on his knees, and lowered his voice. "I got me a play, Bill, one I call RIM. Wanna know why? Because you have to be at the rim-top of your game to execute such a play. Stands for 'runner in motion.' Get it?"

Billy shook his head as he sat down on the sleeping roll.

"*Runner in motion*, Billy. R-I-M. That means a fellow is stealing second base while the batter hits the ball."

Billy grunted, tugging at a boot. He finally yanked it off.

"I got another play," said Jack, lowering to a knee, "I call BRIM. Billy, doggone it, you don't want to even know what this one's all about till you master the other."

"What's it stand for?"

Jack rose, backed way up, then ran forward and slid, boots first, onto his tarp, ending up flat on his back. "*Both* runners in motion," he said. "What do you think about that?"

Billy gave him a slow look from head to toe, then stretched out onto his own roll, dropping his hat onto his face.

Jack guffawed at that, locomotioning with both fists in the air. He could not stay put. Having kept these ideas bound up inside for so long, he was bubbling over at the chance to tell the world's greatest outlaw everything.

"I tell you, Billy, I got baseball plays no one has ever heard of before. That's why I figure by now, with all the special tricks in my arsenal, I'm the world's greatest baseballist in the 'tire nation, bar none." He gave that notion a little consideration, then added, "For my age, that is."

"You got an arsenal of tricks, son," said Billy's hat. "That's for sure."

Jack couldn't quite tell, but he thought he'd heard a mocking tone in Billy's voice. "Well, I happen to possess an active mind. No law against that, is there?"

"Active? Son, you have tall tales running through your head like coyotes chasing chickens all around the roost."

Jack rolled over. *That*, he realized, was no mock. That was admiration. "I can't help it, Billy. It's just how everything comes in and goes out."

Billy lifted his hat and set it on his chest. "And it took me a while to realize that. First I thought you were just a no-good lying cuss. Then I finally saw what all was going on."

Jack rose to an elbow. "You did? What all'd you see, Billy?"

Billy took a moment. "Listen, I don't need to know your life story, Jack Dillon. And believe me, you tell a good one. I just need to know if I can close my eyes around you. And after today, I ain't a-worried on that point any longer."

Jack let out a loud breath and fell back down, savoring those words. "Well, if it helps," he said, "I ain't all that worried about you neither." And he felt as if he were floating amongst the stars.

One week earlier . . .

THE WESTERN UNION TELEGRAM COMPANY

On: April 29, 1881

Received at: Chicago Ill

Date: Apr 30, 1881

To: Wm. Hulbert

Mine rich. Much gold. Team strong.

X measures required. Plans underway.

V. Toots

The moon had set hours before, and in the dark of an early morn, Jack and Billy mounted their horses, then started off along the canyons and ridges to the southwest, toward the Mexican line, searching for a more gradual climb into the steep San Diego mountain country. Jack learned that Billy had spent several years in Mexico, and not only spoke Spanish fluently, but knew the terrain as well. Jack just hoped they would cross a cold-water stream sometime soon so he could refill his water jug and give his face a wake-up soak.

Relying only upon their blue-jean trousers as leg chaps against the stickle-branched chaparral, they pressed on, eventually gaining more altitude as dawn broke behind them and the sunrise began to cast orange and red beams onto the boulder sides ahead.

Not attacking the hills straight on—due west, that is—irritated Jack. "Let's just pick a trail and try it," he'd said, worried that too much time was being lost in seeking a gentler rise.

"Those western trails you see are all dead ends," Billy told him. "Deer and goat scampers, mostly. That's why dipping south is going to be faster. This is where you need to step back, son, and read the mountain. Don't worry, we'll get there."

But when? thought Jack.

As the morning grew light, they trudged farther upslope where the landscape turned greener and lusher, revealing wide mountain vistas to the south that accordioned away from them, one after the other. Silver granite boulders, seen as white spots from the distance, now stood huge as houses amongst the oak trees, juniper, and pyramid pine.

Cresting one rise, Jack spied a lone prospector in the distance walking a burro into a canyon. "Dillontown?" he shouted.

The young man in a floppy blue hat and scroungy overalls stopped and turned. "Ten miles thataway," he called, waving his arm toward the tallest peak on the ridge, "for a hawk. Twenty miles by horse, if you're crazy enough to go to that worthless town."

"Well, we are. Thanks, pardner." Worthless? Why had the man said that?

The news only increased Jack's desire to ride faster. Twenty miles in this rugged, up-and-down country could take all day. He rode ahead of Billy in silence, eyes alert for shortcuts, urging Homer through the scratchweed brush with boot nudges and tisks.

From atop each new rise, Jack could see scattered trails leading off toward valleys and willow springs. Human travelways, some of them. Others carved by wildlife. Small brackish ponds appeared where Jack and Billy watered their rides but not themselves. They saw chimney smoke rise from single-windowed sheds buried halfway into the hillsides and from mud-mortared log huts built under brawny-shouldered oak trees.

Meeting an old-timer, Jack asked again about the road to Dillontown. The haggard man, leading a bony donkey loaded with gear, grinned, showing more gum than teeth through his gray whiskers. "Don't bother yourself, boys. That town's got a death wish." He walked right on past.

Jack turned. "What do you mean, sir? A death wish."

The miner answered into the mountain. "John Dillon's a crazy fool. He shut down the mine. Stopped all sluicing, except by pick or chisel and a puddling tub." He flapped his hand above his head. "Go, go. See for yourself."

Jack stared helplessly at the vast terrain ahead as the rumpled codger and his donkey tramped down the line.

"I don't believe any of it," he told Billy. "Uncle John's no fool."

Billy rode in silence.

Jack spotted more and more gold miners as the morning wore on, their mines set in the underbrush or out in the open with signs of warning posted high.

Next to one wooden door, chained shut across the opening of a mine, a hand-painted, black-lettered sign said, "Trespassers Will Be Shot!" Under that, another one read, "All Survivors Will Be Reshot!"

Jack hurried on, nearly whooping in delight at the excitement of it all.

Packs of wild horses and *burros*, which Billy said had been abandoned over the years by luckless prospectors, began to appear in the far meadows, roaming free, grazing on fresh greens from recent rains.

"I'll be darned," Jack called. "Horses for the picking."

Around noon, the moon rose, waxing still, gaining in size. A good sign, Jack reminded himself. By midafternoon, they overtopped the crest of the range, which Billy judged to be some five thousand feet above the desert floor, and started down the western slope, crossing streams and pine tree stands. Before long, they finally spied the outskirts of Dillontown. On a windy peak along the butte just above, they stood their horses, looking west, downhill, taking in the California gold rush boomtown-turned-baseball-town below.

"There she is!" said Jack, standing in his saddle. "Hew-ta! The town of our dreams, Billy."

Billy did not answer, but his clear blue eyes searched the valley.

Jack was beat, but he was ready to ride on. He leaned over, pulling his hat tight against the wind, and folded his arms atop his saddle horn. Billy drank from his wet canteen, just filled in a nearby stream.

Showing no sign of the urgency Jack felt, Billy lifted his hat and splashed water onto his long curly hair.

"Must be the hardest part of being an outlaw," said Jack. "Sizing up a new place."

"Not really," said Billy, shaking the water from his head. "Most places end up being about the same before long. Hardest part of outlawin' is that you never get to live yourself a regular life."

"Well, that's the point, ain't it?"

Seeing Billy's frown, Jack wished he'd said something else.

"From age fourteen," said Billy, talking into the valley below, "I been on my own. From fifteen, I was on the run, looking over my shoulder every step of the way. That's why I spent two years down in Mexico. Just so I could, in some fashion, live like a normal boy."

A roar from a crowd of people below reached them. Jack squinted.

"Doggone it, Billy, there's a baseball game going on down there this instant!" He whacked Billy's arm with his hat. "Don't know about you, but I'm hungry and thirsty, and I'm ready to go on down to that ball field and take care of that situation. Always plenty food and drink at a ball game."

Just by the tone of Jack's voice, Homer began dancing, turning from side to side.

"You go," said Billy. "I'll hang back up here."

"You will? Oh, right." Jack knew Billy would have to be more cautious, not knowing who or what he'd find in town. But then a surge of thunder bolted through him. "You mean, go down there and scout things out?"

Billy flipped a coin through the air at Jack. "You're my scout, aren't you?"

It was a twenty-dollar gold piece.

"And count your change," Billy added. "Don't take no wooden nickels."

Jack did not answer. He deposited the coin into his pocket and slowly turned back toward the town—with purpose. He stood in his stirrups and clicked his tongue. Homer lunged forward, into the updraft, straight down the steep grade.

Leaning backward with one arm extended, Jack descended the hill, eyeing the baseball square every chance he got. Slowly, it came into clearer view. With a multitude of people surrounding it, the place looked like an open-air market. A game was definitely in progress.

"We gotta hurry, boy," Jack blurted to Homer, who skittered ahead.

Once in town, Jack trotted his horse past an adobe plaza and onto a cross street, muddy from recent rains. The roadway lacked the usual swarm of horses and wagons he'd found in most trail towns. Maybe the town *was* dying. Or, incredibly, maybe folks were all at the game. That's what Jack decided to believe. That everyone who lived here was a baseball joe.

He spied a barbershop called the Yankee Clipper, which sported a baseball bat, painted red and white, as a barber pole. Only a few men appeared on the boardwalk, going in and out of the Mexican *cantinas* and baseball saloons with names like The Come On Inning and The Ball Yard Bar & Grill.

Overtaking an old prospector riding a creaky, slant-wheeled donkey cart, Jack trotted down the lane, past The Top O' the Fifth Cigar Store advertising "beer & sodas, liquors, wines," and "hickory bats" painted in arched lettering, like dove wings, on the high wood facade above its porch. He passed the Hot Corner Café, St. Anthony's Community Church, and the Home Stone Blacksmith & Livery Post.

With a jingo-jamble stirring in his gut, Jack galloped now. He

could not slow down, but fairly raced, fast as he could, until . . .
There it stood. Cradled by two huge wooden grandstands, painted forest green, was the baseball field. Along the back wall of the stands hung a large banner reading "Dillontown National Tourney of Champions."

"Homer," whispered Jack. "It's true, boy. It's all true. We're not in Kansas City anymore."

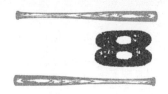

Jack tied Homer to the nearest rail and scrambled around the outer edge of the grandstand on the third-base side. A crowd of spectators, men in shirtsleeves and hats and women hoisting their sun parasols, dripping with fringe, stood ten deep.

"What's the score?" he asked a dapper fellow with his arms folded against his starched white shirt.

"Too much to not enough," snarled the man through a black mustache curtain that drooped below his lips. "Them Dillon-towners has got these Oakland Bay boys tied in knots and stumbling over their own feet. It's nine to four with two innings to go, and the Oakland Mystics are the best challenge team so far. California League champions! I picked them to win and I'm losing a hundred dollars of hard-earned gold dust for the pleasure."

"How many games have I missed?" asked Jack.

"Well, if you're just getting here, son, this is number six, but you'd be stretching your girdle to call any one of 'em much of a contest. Everybody's getting restless. Won't be a real good matchup till those boys from Chicago roll in."

Chicago! thought Jack. It's really going to happen. A match between the Dillontown Nine and the 1880 National League champs.

Jack's original plan had been to compete for a spot on the team well before the tourney had begun. But he'd arrived so late, all he could hope for now was that his uncle, Long John Dillon, would take pity on him, for kinship's sake, and clear him a spot on the team's wooden bench for the final game.

His eyes roamed the field. The sides were changing and the Oakland Mystics were getting ready to bat. Cloaked in striking white uniforms, trimmed in red, they looked a tall and mighty bunch. The home club wore no such vestments. The Dillontown Nine were dressed in the smithereens of baseball knickers or even blue dungarees. Some wore soiled undershirts and half-buttoned jerseys, all stained with either grease or grass. With head and facial hair of varying lengths and states of mattiness, they looked a motley mob. My gosh, thought Jack, feeling disappointed at the lack of glamour.

Their proportions were of every sort, too. Tall thin rails, short squat barrel-shaped men, and those of all size and poundage in between. Rugged prospectors, sure, but to look at them, you'd not suspect they held the agile nature required to play baseball at its highest level.

At shortstop stood Little Lou Montague, the great hitter Jack had read about. Surprisingly, he was hardly as tall as Jack, yet he had batted .451 the previous year. Behind him, warming up in left field, was Shadowfox Coe, a .357 hitter who, folks said, could cover more ground than a windswept brushfire. Jack knew their names and even their stats, but this was the first time he had ever laid eyes on any of them.

At second base, he spotted Jésus de Luz, a slender man who had the tree-trunk arms of a blacksmith, his off-season occupation. He was such a great hitter and swift fielder, the newspapers claimed he could play for any club in the land. The fact that he played second, Jack's strongest position, was not very promising for Jack.

I need to talk to Uncle John, he decided. Pronto. Craning his neck, he searched every player on the field without spotting any likely candidates before realizing that, as player-manager, Uncle John might not be out there on the ball field at all.

"I'm looking for my uncle, sir," said Jack, again turning to the stranger. "Long John Dillon. Do you see him?"

The man looked at Jack with eyes wide and wobbly. "You? You're Long John's nephew?" He blasted out a laugh that parted his mustache.

"Well, now, why is that so darn funny? Yes, sir, I am, and I wish to meet the man." He had waited so long for this moment. He could not falter in his mission now.

The bemused fellow swung his head and used his eyes to indicate Jack's uncle. "He's right over there, my boy. Playing first base."

Jack rose up as high as he could stand to recheck the ballplayer across the field tossing warm-up grounders from first base. He could not believe his eyes. Saying nothing, he decided to retreat from this fellow, who was now having a bigger laugh, and wade back through the crowd to a closer vantage point for a better look.

How could it be, Jack wondered, that with all his reading, all of his planning for this monumental journey, he had never once heard that Long John Dillon was a black man?

This was going to complicate things, he realized. What had he done? Jumped to an early and faulty conclusion based on sharing the man's last name and the few spare hints of background included in newspaper and baseball journal reports? No, of course not. This man *had* to be his uncle.

He continued to work his way through the crowd, careful not to get elbowed or clobbered while the spectators reacted vigorously to a diving stab by the second sacker, de Luz, and his whip to first to make the out.

Jack decided to tuck himself into the walkway between the two grandstands, directly behind the home stone. He sauntered up amongst a few other onlookers while he pondered his circumstance. Can't change my story now, he decided. Besides, somethin' in my bones tells me this baseball man is my father's brother, no matter what he looks like.

All right, then, thought Jack, this here's the hand I've been dealt, so I'll just have to play it.

From his new viewpoint behind the batsman, Jack soon found himself transfixed by the Dillontown hurler, Two-Fingered Dixie Bodine, who actually had three fingers if you counted his thumb. Wounded many years ago, near the end of the Civil War, the young Rebel had later developed a unique release, giving him an unpredictable pitch that darted around like a sparrow hopping branches in a bush.

Dixie Bodine stood at the back of the six-by-six pitcher's box, holding the ball by his side, glaring at the next batter. Then he started his run, sprinting toward the hitter, launching his pitch at the very front line of the box—a side-wheeling, cross-fire fastball with plenty of spin and snap.

The batsman stood steady, eyeing the pitch, then offered a swift swing, slamming the ball high into the sky.

Jack's breath stopped, his mouth agape. What a smash! The Oakland Bay hitter had gotten ahold of this one, that was for sure. Higher and higher it climbed, angling over the left fielder's head.

"Go, Shadowfox, go!" the Dillontown crowd yelled, encouraging their star fielder.

But no matter how fast the Fox ran, Jack could see he was not going to catch up to this one.

Until . . .

Well, it seemed as if a few overzealous spectators, sitting in three rows of rickety old bleacher seats out beyond left field, did not like the looks of that fly ball, home run bound as it appeared to be.

All at once, as if they were in a church choir, five men stood up, drew their pistols, and fired into the hapless baseball, which suddenly dropped like a dying dove into the glove of Shadowfox Coe. The crowd hooted.

"Batter's out!" screamed the umpire.

"Preposterous!" screamed the Mystics manager. "That ball was headed into home-run territory."

"Maybe so," said the umpire, "but doggone, boys, I'll just have to remind you once again. Around here, bullets are part of the playing field. They are a natural occurrence, just like birds."

"Natural?" The poor man circled around in disbelief, his hands hoisted high. "But they shot it out of the sky!"

"Precisely," said the umpire. "They shot it 'out.' If they'd of shot it 'safe,' then yes, you, sir, would have a point." He turned and walked back to the home stone. "Play!"

"*Play?*" Now the Oakland Bayman was steamed. Stomping around the infield with the entire team behind him, he bellowed, "We play under protest, sir! There is a thousand dollars at stake. This is an outrage."

By gosh, thought Jack, I now see how Shadowfox covers so much ground—and why Uncle John's team claimed such a prodigious record. He studied the crowd around him, who were chirping in delight amongst themselves. Was this the way they played ball out here? If so, it wasn't right.

The umpire turned around, facing the grandstands. "Folks, what am I to do?"

"Take your bow, Barnaby," called one man. Others joined him, all shouting the same thing. "Take your bow."

Barnaby, the umpire, wearing a black top hat, waistcoat, and tails, removed his topper, threw his arm across his belly, and bent over into a deep theatrical bow.

The audience rose, laughing and cheering. "Bravo! Bravo!"

To Jack's wonderment, well-dressed merchants and miners alike—some somewhat sober, and some, by looks, fairly sot—roared their approval from the grandstands and slapped the backs of any fellow within striking range until it seemed half a hundred men had tumbled out of their seats and another fifty had swarmed into the stands to replace them.

The umpire then turned slowly toward the mob of enraged Mystics. "We were just joshin', boys. Havin' a little fun. Certainly, that was a home run. The score is now nine to five. There is still only one out in the inning. Play!"

"Well, I'll be darned," said Jack, joining in the crowd's laughter. "How about that?"

A round man in a crumpled white suit across the walkway from Jack fanned himself with his hand. "Typical small-town antics. But let them have their fun. That may be the last ball Mr. Coe has the opportunity to catch."

"Why do you say that?" asked Jack.

The pale man continued to fan his face, turning and staring right at Jack with eyes the size of bullets. "I understand he's a wanted man. A man like him might not even live through the night."

With that, he sucked in his jowls, making a noise not unlike that of a rat eating the yolk from a cracked egg. He slurped his tiny mouth into a tight grin, then slowly waddled away.

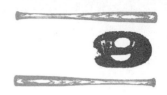

Before play could begin again, the Mystics manager protested again.

"I ask for time," he yelled, pointing to the long home-run ball that had just been returned. "That baseball's in shreds. It's full of bullet holes, and the cover's near ripped off."

Barnaby walked forward and asked to see the ball. Upon examining it, he said, "We can't replace this ball until the end of the inning. That's the rules."

"I know the rules," said the manager. "But you can't even call that a baseball."

Barnaby turned to the crowd and barked, "Seamstress!"

From high in the grandstands a woman hollered. "Dacknabbit! I just got up here and sat down." She rose. "Toss it to me, you long-tailed chimney sweep. That is, if your squeakmouse arm can throw it this far."

The crowd roared. Barnaby, in his top hat, black tails and all, wound up and sailed the flappy ball her way. The feisty seamstress snagged it like King Kelly on a lazy afternoon. The crowd cheered their approval while Barnaby offered instructions.

"Just put the gizzards back in that ball and seam it up, Agnes. That's all I ask."

After a few minutes, the task was done, and the game started again. The wobbly ball, however, confounded the hitters even more as Dixie made short work of the next two Mystics.

The teams changed sides, allowing Jack to get one more look at his uncle as he trotted across the field.

How many John Dillons could there be in California? he wondered. Especially one who'd come from St. Louis in search of gold. Not more than one, Jack felt sure. This man—resemblance or not—was his father's long-lost brother, John. He had to be. Or how else could Jack's dreams ever come true?

"Striker to the line!" yelled Barnaby near the front edge of the crowd, belting out his call for a Dillontown batter to begin the next inning.

Another official, sporting a pointed brown beard and wearing a wide-brim, southern-style hat, called the striker's name.

"Fence Post Hayes!"

And up stepped the shortest, squattiest no-necked ballplayer Jack had ever seen. He certainly never would've guessed Mr. Hayes looked like that. Jack watched him beat the ground a few times with—as far as he could tell—an actual fence post, as tall as the man who held it. Even appeared to have a short length of barbed wire still embedded in the splintered grain.

He called for a pitch right at eye level, and the Oakland Mystics hurler obliged, with a side-slung underhanded whip, sending the ball toward home base at a goodly clip.

The batsman swayed back, then tightened his grip on the

whittled handle, hefted the post off his shoulder, and launched a ferocious attack against the ball, a motion not too unlike a gold miner hammering an iron pick into the sidewall of a mine shaft. Jack figured it was probably how Fence Post Hayes had learned to hit.

The result ended up parting the crowd gathered behind the center-field man as the ball overshot him and tumbled past coyote trails and stony juts well beyond the spectator margins of the field.

Mr. Fence Post Hayes circled the base paths and sauntered across the home stone no more excited or stirred than if he'd just milked a cow.

The announcer in the wide white hat boomed, "Ten runs to five, in favor of the Dillontown Nine."

Watching Fence Post step down into the unusual cellar where the whole team sat, Jack could not help but comment. "I've never heard of such a thing. A team bench plunked down into a hole in the ground."

"That's another one of old John Dillon's newfangled ideas," said a fellow standing just in front of Jack in plush boots and a fancy white shirt. "He's full of them. Supposed to keep the team cool, like down in the gold mines."

"What do they call 'em?"

"Holes in the ground, for all I care!" said the man, returning his gaze to the field. "Bunch of foolishness. In my day, they didn't coddle the ballplayers."

Another man, old and thin, with a face that held the tanned rawhide wrinkles of a thousand smiles, sidled up next to Jack.

"Dugouts," he said in a whispery voice. "They call 'em dugouts. Name comes from that style of canoe the Indians build."

Jack tipped his hat and smiled. "It's a fancy idea."

"I, for one, laddie, wish we had had them in my day. 'Course, most of us would've sat in the desert sun, getting paid no more than two bits a game, and still believed we held the finest employment on God's green earth."

"You played baseball in the olden days?"

"Aye, lad, I played with Alexander Cartwright himself, the Granddaddy of Baseball, back when he ran the old Knickerbockers Ball Club in New York City. I was with him in '49, too, when he came to California, spreading the game across the land."

"My gosh. What is your name, sir?"

"Becket. Thomas Becket." Clean-shaven of cheek, chin, and jowl, he nevertheless had a long beard that flowed like a waterfall from his jawbone on down.

"My name's Jack." They exchanged nods.

"Yes, sir," the old man continued. "Cartwright came here searching for gold. Like everyone else, he thought he'd strike it rich and retire. Never realized he was bringing the gold with him. Well, to be honest, he'd brought diamonds." Mr. Becket winked. "Baseball diamonds."

"Well," said Jack. "I'll be darned."

"Darn tootin'! Now it's all changed. There's gamblers crawling all over the game. Dishonest players. Fixers. Back East, lad, baseball is in a sorry state. Which is why I live right here. The last bastion of honest ball."

Jack considered Mr. Becket's assessment. No wonder ball clubs across the land were closing down. It wasn't just because of a lack of spark. The integrity of the game was disappearing, too—deep into the pockets of gamblers and crooks. And some of them were ballplayers.

Figuring this old-timer may be an asset in his quest, Jack decided to stay friendly. "That there's my uncle. Mr. John Dillon. I've come all the way from St. Louis to meet him. By way of Kansas City. And, uh, Tombstone," he added for flavor.

"Well, you don't say. He's a good man."

"Yes, sir. I'm hoping to join his team."

"Those men think the world of John Dillon, I'll tell you that. And he feels the same way about them. But you may want to put in a few more years of ball playing, my boy, before you step up to this club. I've seen the best players in the nation, and I agree with your uncle's assessment. These men could hold their own on any of the top professional teams. For them to have come together in this small town at this moment in time is nothing, I say, short of a miracle. I'm just grateful to be a witness to it." He gave Jack a quick wink and nod. "I'll take you over to meet him after the game, lad, if you'd like."

"You will? That would be *aces!*"

Suddenly, a great cry and shuffle arose from the dugout of the Dillontown Nine. And from the midst of all that commotion came a snake flying through the air onto the field.

Next came a yell. "I'm bit!"

"Who's bit?" someone said. "What happened?"

Another spectator answered, "That's the rover, Little Lou Montague."

Soon all could see as Little Lou, ace shortstop, hopped out of the dugout toward the playing field, holding one arm aloft and pointing at the snake with the other.

"That dern rattler bit me! Hiding right under the bench board, dag blast it, behind my medicine jug. When I come to fetch a sip, the serpent bit my hand."

As if in response, the rattlesnake coiled up in front of the pitcher's box and rattled its tail for all to hear, loud as a shook gourd.

From across the field, Long John Dillon, now standing in the coacher's box next to first base, called, "How bad did he get you?"

The shortstop stopped short and thought a moment. "Not too bad, I suppose, Cap'n."

Little Lou shook his hand a few times, then looked around and grinned. "Why, it warn't nothin' but a scratch, Cap'n." He turned and strode back to the team bench. He held the bite to his mouth, pulled it away with a smack, then spat on the ground.

"Soon's I get me a dram of tonic down my throat," he announced, "I'll be fit as fine."

The whole ball park hooted at that. One player brought out a white clay jug and gave it to him. The umpire strode toward the snake, pulled out a pistol from inside his coat, and shot the intruder through the head. Calmly, he replaced his gun and started back to his position.

High in the sky, a hawk circled, then swooped. With a curdling cry of *"Kee! Kee!"* the red-tailed hawk fell to the earth, outstretched talons piercing the still-writhing snake on the fly. And off again it flew, into the blue vista, leaving the field as it had been only moments before, save for a small pool of snake blood.

The killer rode in from the east.

Over desert stone and cactus thorns, over bleached-white oxen bones, the gunman climbed out of the desolate sand and rode up the mountain walls with one idea in mind. He was bound to bring a man to justice, though he might die in the trying.

Donned in black leather chaps atop a black-hide steed, he galloped upslope, into the dry hills of chaparral, over a ridge called Rattlesnake, facing the setting sun.

In his eyes, the sun turned cold. On his chest a silver badge flickered red. In his head, visions of murder for money swung high.

He was a simple man. He was the law of the land, a land where murder was often deemed lawful. In fact, a man could be highly rewarded for executing the deed.

From behind, Jack felt someone grip his shoulder with the clutch of an iron vise.

Jack ducked and spun, to pull away from the stealthy claw.

Just as he was about to sprint off, he managed to see it was Billy standing there, freshly dusted if not scrubbed, winking and grinning.

"Doggone it!" said Jack. "What are you doing"—he lowered his voice—"stealin' up on me like some ol' outlaw?" Now he talked through frozen lips. "You're supposed to wait until I finish my observations."

"Got tired of waiting." Billy surveyed his surroundings calmly, seeming to like the box-canyon feel of the walkway. "I've been hearing gunshots for a while, so I figured I'd head down and lend you a hand in whatever trouble you were gettin' yourself into."

"I ain't in no trouble. Everything's just fine." Avoiding Billy's eyes, Jack coughed into his hand.

Billy hummed. "I see." He leaned into Jack's ear. "You know, son. In poker, when a player displays a certain mannerism every time he's bluffing, we call that a 'tell.' And you've got one too. Every time you try to hide the truth, you cough into your hand."

"I do?" He dipped his head. "I never noticed."

Still speaking softly, Billy said, "Now, you neglected to tell me something, didn't you? That your uncle was a freedman from Missouri. A former slave."

Jack blinked a few times, realizing Billy had done some scouting himself. He glanced up once again at the enormous black man clapping his hands in the coacher's box.

"Well, now," said Jack, in a hushed voice, his mind flying into explanation mode. "I thought I did tell you about my uncle.

Don't you remember? I said he was the black sheep of the family."

Billy burst out laughing. "That's not what that saying means."

"Next hitter," called the announcer, "Tonio Wingo."

"Striker to the line," said the umpire.

"All right, all right." Jack could barely watch the game with his mind still whizzing about. "It's not? I mean, I know it's not, but that's just how my family always put it." He looked out again, then down at his hands, fighting the urge to lift one and cough into it.

"Fact is," Billy continued, "he ran away from his owner when he was only fifteen. Up the Mississippi. It's a pretty good story."

"It is," Mr. Becket agreed, joining in. "Landed up in Keokuk, Iowa, where he stayed till the end of the war."

"You don't say," said Jack. "Billy—uh, Bill Henry, I'd like you to meet Mr. Becket, a fine baseball man. He knows my uncle, too."

Billy touched the brim of his hat.

Mr. Becket nodded.

"I heard tell," said Billy, "that Long John Dillon owns five hundred head of cattle."

"Oh, maybe in days gone by, lad," said Mr. Becket. "Now he's down to a couple of milk cows, I'd say."

"What about his *hacienda*?" asked Billy. "Know where that is?"

Jack cringed.

"If that's what you want to call it . . ." Mr. Becket grinned. "Happens to be in the middle of town. It's that Touch 'Em All pub house."

"It is?" Jack spun to look. "He lives in a saloon?"

"Aye, he does, lad. Lives upstairs in a big hotel suite built just for him. He owns the place. Used to own half the town. But hard times hit, so now he's down to a section of land up on the ridge and the Lucky Strike Gold Mine. Which, I must say, did pretty well for the man. Out of nine local strikes, it turned out to be the largest one around. Aye, but he hasn't pulled any gold out of it in more than two years."

"Doggone, son," said Billy. "Nothing about your Uncle John story seems to be going your way."

"*My* story? You think I made this all up? I grew up hearing all this." Jack once again studied his bare arm. "'Sides, his skin's not that much darker'n mine. And looks can be deceiving, Billy. Look at yourself, for example. You don't exactly have 'wanted desperado' written all over—" He stopped.

He froze cold, realizing he'd just let slip something he should've kept secret. Billy lowered his head and leaned against the green wooden skirt of the stands. But even with his eyes aimed at the ground, Jack felt their burn.

"Well, of course you don't," Jack said, acquiring a jolly tone. "Why would you? But on the other hand, look at me. Who'd take me for being the grandest authority and soon-to-be greatest practitioner of a spanking new style of professional baseball in all the land—but I am."

"You got yourself a point there." Billy caught Mr. Becket's eye, sending him a wry smile. "Nobody'd take him for that, now, would they?"

The old man wheezed out a laugh and turned back to the game.

Jack folded his arms, staring harshly, hoping to regain a bit of dignity. Seeing a Dillontown batter thrown out at first and the teams beginning to change sides, he moved to refocus the conversation back to the game.

"Last inning coming up," he said. "Top of the ninth."

Billy hummed, seeming relieved the game was winding down.

Jack watched the Dillontown Nine rise from the dugout bench. All except Little Lou, who did not even move.

"Doc!" one player called. "Where's Doc Hathaway?"

"At the saloon, where else?" came a reply.

"Better go get 'im. Little Lou is turning blue."

Little Lou fell over. Other men turned back and rushed to his aid.

Seeing as how Doc Hathaway never did appear, they eventually carted the shortstop off on a flat-wagon. Little Lou's position on the field was taken by Lefty Wright, a backup pitcher. But the game was far enough along and the scores far enough apart that it hardly mattered.

From the Oakland side a few spectators tried to fire their team up. "Now, boys, show a little ginger out there! Rup, rup, now. Show us some pluck."

But as the game resumed, it became apparent that the Northern Californians were plain out of pluck. Their first batsman missed two quick pitches, then hit an easy squibber back to Dixie. One dead, two to go.

Billy became distracted. He appeared more interested in staring off toward the mountains than following the action. Before the next batter stepped up, Jack followed Billy's gaze into the hills.

In the distance, a horseman was approaching.

Jack saw nothing outstanding about the rider, dressed in black, until a flash caught his eye. Something on the horseman's chest glittered in the afternoon light.

"Marshal's coming," said Mr. Becket.

"Yep," said another man. "That's Danbridge."

"Who's he?" asked Jack.

"U.S. marshal out of Tombstone. Hasn't been this way in months."

"Must be serious."

Others joined in the speculation. "Serious money, more like. These days, it seems he's a lot keener on hunting bounties than marshalin'."

"Slim pickins in this town for a bounty hunter," said another. "I don't know of anyone with a price on his head worth riding across that desert for."

"Maybe not," said Mr. Becket. "But I'd place a handsome wager that our lad Danbridge does."

Working slowly over the rocky terrain, horse and rider made their way toward the outfield throng, then amongst them, cutting straight through the crowd of women, children, and hard rock miners.

Most men in the stands stood to watch. Some moved closer to the field. Quietly, Billy sidled off behind Jack and a cluster of gawkers. In two steps, he was gone.

Jack peered after Billy, but soon lost all trace. Mr. Becket noticed Billy's quick departure as well.

"Your friend, Bill Henry," he said, nodding toward town. "Seemed a wee bit jumpy."

Jack gave Mr. Becket a big grin, hoping to hide the fact that this wise old baseball man had seen more than Jack thought. "Oh, him? He's just antsy to find himself a good poker match, is all. Not much of a baseball joe. And he doesn't like staying in one place too long. That's all."

"Well." The old man folded his arms against his chest, looking straight ahead. "Desperados never do."

Jack's mouth fell open, and he used the opportunity to generate a huge laugh. "That's a good one, Mr. Becket. Ol' Bill Henry, a desperado. He's desperate, all right, trying to get himself a job around here as a . . . as a schoolteacher."

Mr. Becket did not respond.

The game had come to a halt. The marshal, dressed in a black vest draped with a silver pocket chain, rode almost to second base, then stopped.

"What do you think you're doing?" bellowed Long John Dillon, who had gone to the dugout and retrieved a baseball bat during the commotion.

The lawman called to the crowd. "I have a warrant—"

"I don't care if you have the Ten Commandments and your name is Moses!" Long John shouted. "I'll not stand for this." Waving the bat over his head, he strode right for the marshal. "Get off this here field! This is a baseball game, and it is sacred. You have no right to halt this affair."

The marshal drew his rifle and pointed it. "Stay put, Dillon. A baseball bat is no match for one of these. Loses every time."

John Dillon pulled up, slapping the bat barrel into the palm of his massive hand, but he did not argue the point.

"That goes for all of you." The marshal scanned the crowd with a fierce glower. "I'm not afraid to use this. Now, as I was saying, I have a warrant for the arrest of Robert 'Shadowfox' Coe, on a charge of first-degree murder."

Instantly, Shadowfox tore off running for the foul line. Danbridge took note and galloped after him and, with the stock end of his rifle, struck Shadowfox in the head. The blow sent the accused man ragdolling across the dirt and into a dusty heap. Knocked out cold.

The stunned crowd issued no more than a low "whoa."

John Dillon turned his back and walked away.

The marshal dismounted. After placing a boot heel on Shadowfox's neck, Danbridge bent down and tightened a pair of iron cuffs to the fallen man's wrists. Next, he hefted him shoulder high and laid the limp prisoner facedown across his saddle.

U.S. Marshal Danbridge then walked his horse off the field, circled around the crowd, and headed for town.

Once more, Jack spun in search of Billy. No sign. He'll take care of himself, Jack decided. It's the marshal who should be worried.

Glancing back at the bustle on the field, Jack watched as players shifted around yet again to fill another empty spot. He saw Lefty, the rover, leave his position at shortstop to become the third outfielder. Noticing that there was no one left on the Dillontown bench, Jack suddenly had a convolutionary idea.

"I do appreciate your offer to introduce me, Mr. Becket, sir, but I believe I'd better go right now to let my uncle know I'm in town."

He darted off toward his newfound relation. Through the crush of spectators, Jack wove his way to the edge of the Dillontown dugout. He needed to tell his uncle not to worry, to tell him there was one top-notch replacement player ready and raring to go.

But Jack was not the first to arrive. He fell in behind a gaggle of men, pressing together, who all had the same idea. John Dillon stood with his back turned, setting the bat he had wielded into an old wooden barrel before retaking his position on the field.

"I'm here to help, Mr. Dillon," said the closest fellow. "I run like a rabbit and hit like King Kelly."

The next fellow pushed that man aside. "I'm another Cap Anson. As sure-handed an infielder as you're gonna find, but I can perform in any spot."

"I, too," called out a man behind him. "I am a trained ballist. From Rochester, New York." Several others chimed in on a similar note. "Providence," said one man. "Cincinnati," declared another.

"Kansas City!" shouted Jack from behind them all. "Uncle John! It's me, Jack Dillon, your nephew!"

Finally, this was enough to make John Dillon respond. He withdrew the bat from its barrel and cracked it against the pine-log roof of the dugout. The whole gang fell silent.

"Who do you fools think you are? There is only one out until this ball game is over. I just lost two good men—men I cannot afford to lose—to unnatural circumstances, and you swarm in here like buzzards to a deer kill. If I should be in need of ball-players, I shall let it be known. Even with eight men on the field, our team is stronger than most, and it shall prevail." He tossed down the bat and waved his tree-trunk arms. "Now be gone, the lot of you! Don't be comin' 'round here, a-worryin' me with foolishness." He trotted onto the field.

Jack stood stunned. *Foolishness?* Risking the big man's ire, Jack shouted back, "But I'm your nephew from Missouri. Patrick Dillon's son. I have baseball in my blood, sir, same as you."

Halfway to his position at first base, Long John Dillon came to a halt. He slowly turned around, gave Jack a fierce look, then shook his head with a growl and turned away.

After the game, Jack led his horse to the Home Stone Blacksmith and Livery Post to get Homer properly settled, curried, and fed. Once inside the huge barn doors, he saw a circular adobe-brick forge, full of smoldering coke. Mounted on a tree trunk nearby stood a large iron anvil, well used, judging by its saddlebacked strike face.

A dark-eyed girl approached from the horse stalls in the rear.

"Excuse me," said Jack. "I need to put up my horse."

The girl smiled. She wore a leather smock over blue denim pants tucked into rawhide boots, and a boy's shirt, once white, now stained with the soot of the blacksmith's coal. Jack was entranced.

"I am Eliza," she said with a strong Mexican accent. Perspiration dampened her forehead, as if she'd just recently been using the smithy's forge. "I will take care of him for you."

Jack nodded, feeling for a moment that he could do nothing but stand there and look at her.

Her large eyes painted over him as well. Then she approached

Homer, and her eyes grew even larger when she spotted the bat handle sprouting from the saddle.

"You," she said to Jack. "You play baseball?"

"I do," he said, nodding and grinning. "I'm Jack Dillon, out of Kansas City, Missouri. Mr. Long John Dillon's long-lost nephew himself."

"*¿Qué?*" She now seemed alarmed. "You are Señor Dillon's nephew?" She glared into Jack's face, her eyes prospecting, looking for clues.

"I know we may appear—I mean, it's hard to see the resemblance between us right off, but, you see, we come from a very large family."

Eliza smiled, giving Jack a firm nod, as if she knew all about large families. "*Sí,*" she said, "of course. You come to play baseball?"

"Yes, I did, indeed."

"The boys have many teams in this town."

"Oh, no. Not with the boys. With the men! I am one crackerjack ballplayer, and I intend to lend my uncle a hand whipping those fellows from Chicago."

She lowered her eyes, not seeming to believe such bluster from a boy.

"The baseball games, *ay,* they are *muy importante.*" She took in a deep breath that returned as a sigh.

"Well, I know," said Jack. "Ten thousand dollars is a lot of money."

"*Ay, sí,*" she said. "But it is more than this. The town of your uncle—Dillontown—one time it was full of many people and much money. Then the gold was big. Now it is small. You do not know this?"

"Well, sure I do. But, I mean, not exactly." He narrowed an eye.

"The streams, they are picked clean. And in the hills, the miners have taken all they can with pick and shovel. By hand, they cannot go more deep to get any more gold. The only way is to *es*-plode the mountain."

"Would they do that?"

"*Sí,* of course. Some say inside the mountain is one million dollars, maybe more. As much as the hills have given already. But finding this gold means breaking the mountain apart *con neetro-glee-serena.*"

"Nitroglycerine?"

"*Sí.*" She nodded with vigor, sending the single braid down her back horsetailing back and forth. "And then they wash the broken mountain into the rivers and valleys with hoses of strong water. This is why the baseball games, they are so important."

"I still don't quite follow."

"Some people want Señor Dillon to break his mountains. But he say no. It is wrong. And that makes a war in this town."

"It does?" Jack swiftly glanced around the barn. "You need a couple of gunslingers?"

"No, no. Not this kind of war. At least, not yet."

He cocked his head. "What kind?"

She stepped closer. "A war of dreams. I show you." She

glided back, using the barn floor as if it were a stage, and brought a hand to her chin. "When the gold digging slows down, the people think and think what to do."

Eliza then placed her hands on her hips and faced the wall. "Half, they say, 'Are we going to dig holes in this rock-hard land until we crawl into one and die? Or do we buy cattle and plant this land full of vital greens and apple trees and play baseball all year long?'

"Then these people, they say this." She jumped up and spun around to portray the other side, using a hoarser voice. "'It's gold we want, dang-nabbit! And we can *blast* away for it.'"

Jack fought hard to hold back a grin. He did not want to insult this intriguing girl or halt her captivating performance.

Eliza continued. "So the first, they say, 'Apples are filled with *liquid* gold, and trees give fruit year after year.' The yelling, it would go on far into the night."

"So what do *you* say?"

"Señor Dillon dreams to make Dillontown the greatest baseball town in the world." Eliza threw her hands high. "A heaven of baseball. I agree. Baseball is this town's best hope. I say, cows give us milk, cream, and butter. Apples bring us the apple pies. With baseball, ice cream, and apple pie, who needs gold?"

At that very moment, Jack felt that perhaps, not for sure, but maybe, this brown-skinned, brown-haired, wide-eyed girl had said the most wonderful words he had ever heard.

"I agree," he blurted. "I agree one hundred and ten percent. I was on the verge of saying the very same thing myself, in fact, when I couldn't decide between apple pie and apple strudel." His boots scratched nervously into the soft dirt. "But I was leaning toward pie."

Eliza smiled at Jack, showing bright teeth and a hint of dimples. She stepped forward and took the reins from him. "Now, I care for your horse."

"*Gracias*, Eliza. That would be mighty fine." He reached into his pocket and dug out Billy's coin.

"Here," he said. *"Muchas gracias."* He pressed the gold coin into her hand. As he did, his fingertips brushed her palm, and he felt a shock, one that emptied every thought from his brain.

She looked down at the gold piece, then smiled into his eyes. *"De nada."*

Realizing he was not moving, was only staring, and maybe drooling, he spun around and started to leave. But before reaching the door, he stopped himself with a slide. He quickly walked back to her.

"Oh, I almost forgot. Did a fellow just come through here, blond, curly hair, drover's hat, with a look on his face like he could be some sort of desperate outlaw who's sorely missing his sidekick and scout?"

Eliza pointed to Billy's horse, which Jack only now recognized, against the far wall, freshly brushed and eating oats. "*Sí, pero* his face showed me only a smile."

"I'll bet. Be careful of that *hombre*. Did he say what he was up to?"

"He say he is hungry." She assumed a casual, crooked stance like Billy's and lowered her voice. "He say, 'Eliza, I need to find a good *cantina*—and a good game of poker.'"

She hurried past Jack to the stable door. "I show him the *cantina* of my *tia*, Rosa. Then I tell him Papa always plays cards at the Touch 'Em All Saloon." She pointed out both establishments.

"Eliza, thank you *muy, muy* much. And you watch. I plan to join my uncle's team, and I plan to be a big help in making this town the heaven of baseball, just like you said." Giving her one last glance, he decided to ask one last question. "How old are you?"

She stood before him, as if at attention, with a dignified air. "I am fourteen."

Jack lowered his voice as deep as it would go. "I am, too," he told her, then strode slowly out the open door and coughed into his hand.

Nine days earlier . . .

April 28, 1881

My dear Captain Dillon,

Greetings from Chicago. Thank you for your persistence in this matter. Yes, I do believe the new terms you have suggested will make our contest <u>all the more interesting</u>. I hereby agree to those terms set forth in your final proposal, as follows:

- Each club will put up $10,000, cash or gold, as prize money, the total to be awarded to the winning team.
- In addition, Mr. Dillon, you agree to put at stake your ownership of the Lucky Strike Mine, to be awarded to me in the event our team prevails.
- In the event your team prevails, I promise to use my authority as president of the National League of Professional Base Ball Clubs to appoint your club, the Dillontown Nine, to fill the spot recently vacated by the Cincinnati Red Stockings for the 1881 season.

Yours truly,
William Hulbert
Owner, Chicago White Stockings

Jack searched the Touch 'Em All Saloon first. The place was crawling with roughnecks and bouncing with piano music. He passed several three-card monte games, where dealers swirled the facedown cards around on the red felt tabletops like bartenders pushing a polishing rag, challenging the bettors to keep track of each move.

One dealer, dressed in a frilly white shirt and wearing a small green derby propped sideways on his bald head, kept saying in a deep Irish brogue, "Her', ther', and yon, boys. Hither and yon. Keep a quick eye on the queen, boys. Tell me where she's gone."

Reaching the upright piano along the saloon's back wall, where he figured Billy would most likely be, Jack scouted about and finally spotted him—across the room at a card table in the *front* corner. Sitting near the window with his back to the wall, Billy looked to be winning, too, judging by the stack of gold coins at his chest.

Jack began retracing his steps along the bar when he heard a bone-shaking voice call out. *"Boy!"*

He froze.

"Come back here," bellowed Long John Dillon, standing near the huge mirror. "I want to talk to you."

"You do?" Jack tried to say, and would've said, clearly, had there been half a breath left in his lungs. Instead, his throat collapsed and his legs jellied under him while he flash-pondered what to do next.

Well, Jack decided, meeting Long John Dillon was the reason he was here. If it's do-or-die time, he might as well do this now or die in the trying.

"Yes, sir," said Jack, forcing himself to give the man a big ol' smile.

With a cold stare, John Dillon pointed to the end of the bar. "Meet me over there, near the door."

Jack started moving again, managing to struggle his way through the crowd until he met Mr. Dillon out past the bar top, under the bleached-bone skull of a longhorn steer mounted through the eyeholes to the wood-paneled wall.

"Follow me." Long John Dillon turned to the staircase behind the bar. Jack followed, climbing the stairs, feeling like a condemned man heading for the gallows.

As he climbed, Jack's boots sank into plush red carpet. It seemed to be a house of luxury. At the landing, they followed a hallway that led to an enormous wooden door.

While the big man pulled out his keys, Jack took a long look at the tall oak door, the size of a dining room table. It was carved full of mountains and trees and fat little angels blowing trumpets at a huge, half-globe baseball planted directly beneath a small brass baseball bat serving as a knocker.

Long John Dillon led him into the front parlor. There, stately wooden furniture upholstered in colorful embroidered fabric graced a red-, black-, and white-striped native rug placed over a dark wood floor.

Pointing to an overstuffed chair near a small serving table, Cap'n Dillon said, "Tom Becket tells me I should hear you out. Have a seat."

Jack hesitated because it seemed to be the best seat in the house, but when Uncle John sat in one of two tall-back chairs across the room, Jack decided to sit as well.

The big man took a big breath. "Now, son, you tell me that you are my nephew from Kansas City. And I have to tell you, I have no known nephews, and I sure don't have one from Kansas City."

"Oh, right," said Jack, realizing he had named the last town he'd lived in. "I meant St. Louis."

"St. Louie, Missourah?" barked Uncle John, making it sound more like a threat.

Softly, Jack answered. "Yes, sir?"

John Dillon squinted, cocking his head to the side. "Tell me some more."

"Well, all right." Jack cleared his throat. "We, uh, you see, before Kansas City, we lived in a little town outside St. Louie." He checked the man for a reaction. His face was still frozen cold, but in those icy eyes, Jack thought he saw a flicker of light. "La Croix?"

"Croy Town?"

"Well, um, right across the tracks. I mean, Croy and Croix, they both sound the same, don't they?"

"But they ain't."

"No, sir. But that was where I attended school, La Croix, uh, Town, and played lots of baseball, which was all I ever dreamed about, sir. And I soon grew a fervent desire to visit with you, a baseball man of great renown."

John Dillon sat back, never lifting his eyes. "I did have folks in those parts. Far as I know they may yet be." He adopted a slightly more cordial tone. "So you're trying to tell me that my kid brother, Packy, is your father?"

Oh my gosh, thought Jack. *So* close. "Well, yes, sir. Though some folks call him . . . Patrick?" He smiled, crossing two pairs of fingers on each hand—the old La Croix double double-cross—for good luck.

John Dillon rose to his full height, all fifteen feet of him, plus a boulder of a chest, or so it seemed. "Patrick Dillon, huh?"

"Yes, sir."

"Stand over near that sconce yonder," commanded the man.

Jack swallowed hard, removed his hat, then quickly made his way into the glow of a globed kerosene lamp mounted on the wall.

Long John Dillon walked a semicircle around him. He said nothing, giving Jack a full inspection.

At long last, he grunted. "Doggone, I took you to be Mexican or perhaps Italian. But, snakes alive, if I don't find a trace of my young brother in your face. I have seen that boy only once in more than twenty years." He perused a moment longer. "What did he go and do, up and marry a white woman?"

"Well, sir," said Jack, lifting his shoulders. "You know how love is. I mean, if I'm not being too presumptuous."

Breaking into a crooked smile, Uncle John said, "Listen to you talk. 'Presumptuous.' That is Packy Dillon through and through."

"Yes, sir, that's what I've been trying to tell you."

"And you made your way clean out here all on your own?"

"Yes, sir. For the most part."

"How in the world did you find me, way up here in these hills?"

This one was easy. "You're in all the newspapers, sir."

His eyes widened. "Is that a fact?"

Jack threw his hands up. "This town. This Tournament of Champions. Back East, they think you've got a wagonload of gumption."

John Dillon reared his head back and laughed, laughed as if he'd been saving one up for a long time. "Well, boy, we will soon see what I have here—and who's got the gumption." He wagged his head side to side, gusting out more sharp bursts of laughter. "I have heard some tall tales in my time . . . But I will say this. You do have a glimmer of my young brother in your eyes. Plain as day."

"Well, now, some folks, I'm sure, would say that, sir."

The big man returned to his chair across the room to sit facing Jack. "We may be kin," said John Dillon. "We may not. To be honest, son, I'm not putting a whole lot of stock in anything I've heard thus far."

"Yes, sir." Jack lowered his head.

"But we may, now. We just may." John Dillon folded his arms. His firm, gruff voice had gentled. "I know what it's like to be a boy out alone in this world. So *that* we have in common. Being on constant guard, living by your wits. My father, which would be your grandfather, son." He paused to let Jack glance up and see his earnest gaze. "My father was sold by our master in the St. Louie Square to a white man down in Texas for two hundred dollars when I was but a boy of eight. Packy would've been three. And we never saw him again. Did you know about that, son?"

"No, sir." Jack shifted forward to the edge of his padded seat. Having been orphaned since the age of eleven himself, Jack knew the loss this man must have felt. "I'm sorry, sir. Terrible sorry."

A wash of ancient thoughts appeared to have glazed over John Dillon's face. But they did not last, as if he were used to shaking them off.

"You know, back when I landed out here, sixteen years ago, this valley was nothing but ky-yotes, oak trees, and wild sage. Home to maybe two hundred Kumeyaay Indians living in stick huts. But in two years' time there were five thousand men crawling these hills, all hoping to become millionaires. All on account of a few gold nuggets I happened to stumble upon in the river-bed. Now most of those men are gone. Washed out. And of these folks who are still around, most of them are not here for the gold. They are here for the beauty of this land and the thrills of our ball club, and what these things might provide for them and their families and their souls."

"I understand," said Jack, and it was the truest thing he had said in a long time. The land—this great, vast, unsheltered, windswept, and weather-whittled earth—had been his only real home for the past year. And baseball had been his reason for living.

"This is pure heaven to me," Jack continued. "Boulder mountains, green pastures, peaceful river flowing through. It's a paradise to live in or see, far as I'm concerned."

"But not everybody sees it that way." The gruff voice had returned.

"How do they see it?"

"Some folks look at it as no-good, empty brushland with buried treasure inside, just waitin' for the takin'. They see it as a place to invade, to plunder for its riches, then pack up, move on, and leave it behind, full of gaping wounds. De-treed, de-flowered, and destroyed. And I see this ball game as my last battle against those kinds of men." He laughed. "John Dillon's Last Stand, I reckon. I either slow down the destruction of these hills, the poisoning of these rivers and streams, and establish Dillontown as a year-round baseball heaven full of grazing land, apple trees, and ballparks, or I give up and move on myself."

"Move on? You really would? Where would you go?"

"Don't know. Mexico, maybe. Someplace where a good life is still more important than money."

John Dillon resumed his seat, his eyes again taking on a distant cast.

"My father," he began once more, "even though I lost him at a young age, he gave me a great gift. 'Go, chile,' he said, 'go, chile. Run if you can.' He built a fire inside of me. Five years later, I was sold down the river myself. But I would not stand for it. I was bought by a slave trader in Loozyana and hustled off in chains, bound for New Orleans. But I did not go on that boat."

He rose again. "No, sir! I took a huge risk. But I was young and I was ready to tangle with anyone." He smacked his fists together.

"That night I escaped into the streets of St. Louie and ran to find a man I'd only heard about in crazy late-night tales. But the stories were true. Stories about folks who ran what they called the Underground Railroad.

"They had a whole system back then, and it was white folks and black. This here fellow got me all the way up to Iowa Territory. I landed in the town of Keokuk and was taken in by a family of Quakers. The year was 1855. I was thirteen years old, son, and I stayed in that town for nearly ten years, all through the great Civil War. I learned to read and write and speak the King's English. But most of all, I played ball. During the war, I joined the Southern Iowa Border Brigade, a band of men guarding Iowa from any Missourah Confederates trying to cross over. Or from slave owners set on heading north and gathering up their runaways."

Now Jack was lost in this man's world, standing next to him

in the grass fields of Iowa, playing baseball and guarding the land.

"'Course, most times," he continued, "the border was quiet. We spent many a day playing ball. And when the war ended in '65, I was twenty-three and free to go anywhere in the land, to follow my biggest dream, which was to play top-notch professional baseball. But I soon saw that would require playing games in towns such as St. Louie, Cincinnati, Louieville, and the like. Slave towns. Angry and hateful towns. And I vowed that I would never go back, never step one foot into slave country again."

He took a huge breath and lowered himself back down into his chair. He seemed exhausted from his tale.

"Well, sir, I don't blame you," said Jack, which was all he could think to say.

But, as if he felt bound to explain himself, Uncle John added a last thought. "You see, it ain't just the memories that bother me about slave country. The beatings, the whippings, the constant grief. No, sir. It's the people. The plain fact that I'd be living amongst so many people who saw no problem whatsoever with slavery. People who fought a war, in fact, to keep it alive."

He hung his head.

"It is why I love this game, son. The Cubans are playing it these days. Rico Del Rey, our right fielder. And Mexicans, Indians. Jésus de Luz, Tonio Wingo, Blackjack Buck. Blacks and whites. All Americans can play. That's what's so beautiful about baseball." He shook his head in earnest. "Until it turns corrupt."

"You mean the fixers, the crooked players. I heard about

them. But you don't have to worry. Not out here. That's what Mr. Becket said."

"Mr. Becket does not know what I've done, son." He rose and stepped to the glass doors leading to the balcony over the street. Into the lacy-curtained windows, he said, "The risk I've taken with this one ball game against those Chicago boys. It is bigger than anyone around here knows. And after what I saw happen today, I believe to my bones that I may have tangled with the wrong folks."

Four days earlier . . .

THE WESTERN UNION TELEGRAM COMPANY

On: May 2, 1881

Received at: Tucson, Arizona Territory

Date: May 2, 1881

To: U.S. Marshal Chaney Danbridge

Shadowfox Coe wanted killer member Dillontown Calif baseball team. Will pay triple reward for hasty dispatch. Wire back. Yours,

V. Toots Vice Pres. Chicago Coal Co.

Downstairs again, Jack made his way to Billy's poker table with haste. Before speaking a word, he used his eyes to convey urgency.

Billy caught the signal. "I see my associate has arrived," he said, addressing the table. "Gentlemen, I look forward to resuming our game at a later date."

"Wait a dad-gum minute," called one roughneck, whose stringy black hair draped over the shoulders of his fringed leather vest.

One of the town ballplayers, Fence Post Hayes, was sitting across from Billy. In a soothing tone he told the other cardsharp, "Now hold on. He's free to go, ain't he?"

"Is that what you figure on doing?" said a more dapper fellow wearing a black ribbon tie. "You fixing to take our money and run?"

Billy lowered himself back into the chair. "Easy now, boys. I ain't goin' far. And judging by the competition I'm facing here, believe me, I shall return."

The men relaxed. "Well, that's more like it," said Mr. Fringe Vest. "See that you do, Slick."

Fence Post sent him a friendly wink.

Billy rose more slowly this time, but before he could finish sweeping the gold into his hat, another man was already in his seat, calling, "Deal 'em!" It appeared to be a lively game.

"I sure hope you know what you're doing," said Jack in a hushed tone as they shuffled away to a more private spot. "Out in the open like that? Antagonizing those fellows like that?"

Billy calmly stuffed the coins he'd won into his front pockets. Steering Jack along, he headed for the swinging doors. They stepped outside.

Donning his hat, Billy said, "Look, son, I do not spend my life holing up in the hills, contrary to what you may think. Should I ever need to, I can disappear with the best of 'em. But my style has always been what I call 'hiding in plain sight.' It has served me well for many years and put far more friends on my side than enemies against me. And before too long, I trust those boys will be on my side as well."

Jack did not know how to respond to that, but he did anyway. "Well—well, what about this marshal? Why did you disappear when he showed up?"

"I crossed paths with Danbridge long ago. He was a cattle rustler in those days, a horse thief, too, and a few other things. Since then, he's made a habit of hiring on as sheriff at cow town after cow town, generally those in need of a freewheeling gun-slinger to keep the populace in line. Last we met up was in Dorado, outside Silver Springs, and he marshaled our bunch right down the trail."

"He used to be an outlaw?"

"Most of 'em are. That badge just lets 'em kill without strings. He would've gunned down Shadowfox and saved himself some trouble if no one had been watching."

"Well, doggone, how can you tell the good guys from the bad?"

"Takes practice."

Jack shook his head in wonder.

As they tromped down the boardwalk, Billy checked over his shoulder from time to time and into each doorway they passed.

"So, what do we do now, Billy? Want me to shadow the *hombre*? Spy on his movements?"

"No, no. We let him pass on through. He did his job. Earned a couple hundred dollars. He'll want to cash that in." Billy swatted Jack across the chest with the back of his hand. "Hungry? I was told about a great little place. And besides, I got something to tell you."

"Well, I got something to tell you, too. Let's go."

In Tia Rosa's Cantina, plucked chickens hung from the rafters alongside fresh quarters of beef, hog, and wild goat. Bunches of bright red and green peppers strung with twine dangled between them.

Entering, Jack was overwhelmed by the moist and spicy air. Pinto beans percolated in an iron cauldron while meat sizzled on a huge black grill next to a griddle where corn and flour *tortillas* bubbled as they cooked.

"*Hola*," said Billy, calling to the perky young woman in a long white apron behind the sweet-bread counter. "*Una chica bonita, Eliza, nos envió*. Are you Tia Rosa?"

"*Ay*. Are you hungry?"

"*Sí. Mi compadre* and I need a plate of meat and beans, *por favor*."

The slender woman, not much older than Billy, with wild layers of wavy black hair tied down by a blue bandana, peeked over the counter to locate Jack. She sent him a twinkle-eyed smile.

Jack touched the brim of his holey hat. "Ma'am."

Walking to the rear of the crowded eatery, Billy found a pinetop table away from the other patrons and sat facing the door. Jack took the spindly wooden chair opposite him.

Noticing Billy's ease with Spanish, Jack started off with a question. "How was it for you, living down in Mexico?"

"Mexico? *Fantástico*, most of it." He flashed a squirrelly grin. "Got along good. Mexican people are simple and honest and generous." He stared off with unfocused eyes. "The girls"—he paused to glance toward the griddle, as if he could see Rosa behind the rack of sweet breads—"are pretty. And happy. But you start missin' folks. I noticed it mostly at night. My ma had been dead only a year or so. My brother—who knows where he drifted off to? But I had plenty of friends. *Muchachos buenos*. Shepherds. Goatherds. *Vaqueros*. They were always very good to me."

"Did you have a girl?"

"Lots of girls." That made him laugh, then lower his head as a boyish blush rose up. "You mean a special one?"

Jack widened his eyes.

"Sure," said Billy. "But she's on this side. Back in New Mexico." He tapped the tabletop nervously, then rubbed his hands together. "Anyhow, to the topic at hand. First of all, you're in luck, son. Your so-called Uncle John has done all right for himself."

"I told you," said Jack. "The town's named after him, ain't it?"

Billy's eyes roamed widely as two men entered and took the last empty table near the front window. "Well, you told me lots of things, didn't you? Such as that mighty house he lives in. Not exactly what I pictured."

Tia Rosa appeared with two plates of meat slathered in a steaming dark sauce next to a pile of beans and hot *tortillas*.

"Boy!" said Jack. *"Muchas gracias."*

"De nada." Rosa placed a brown bottle of sarsaparilla in front of each of them. Billy gave her a big smile. She paused to study the table a moment longer, then walked away.

"Well, I tried to tell you, Billy," Jack confided. "Now, I didn't reveal everything on account of I didn't know how you'd take it. Him being a runaway slave and all."

Jack tore apart a buttery corn *tortilla*. He plopped a forkful of meat and beans onto one half, rolled it up, then brought it to his mouth.

"His background don't bother me. I have more in common with him and his run for freedom than you might suppose."

Jack saw the connection and nodded. "All right, that's true. Did you learn anything else?"

Billy grunted, swallowing a bite. "There is a prophet on the team."

"A what?"

"An honest-to-goodness future-dreaming man of prophecy. He's the catcher, Blackjack Buck."

Jack pondered this news a moment. "You don't really think a fellow can see the future, do you?"

"Apparently this fellow can." Billy tore off a *tortilla* slice, using it to swipe up some beans. "Not only that, he delivers his prophecies in poems."

"In poems?" Jack was immediately curious.

"And they rhyme," said Billy. "Perfect English, better than the guy speaks."

"That's spooky."

Billy dabbed at the sauce around his beef. "But here's the biggest news. Your uncle walked into the bar today, slammed his hands down on the bartop, and announced that he's been forced to hold a tryout for two replacement players on his team. Tomorrow morning, ten o'clock."

Jack opened his mouth in awe. "He did? I didn't even ask him about a tryout. I was too scare—I mean, I was too scatterbrained by the time we finished reminiscing and all." He looked up at the bright blue, red, and brown village fresco painted on the wall, seeing it now for the first time. "That's the chance I've been waiting for, Bill Henry."

"Thought you'd say that. He said they're facing the Chicago White Stockings in two days, and he needs a good solid team."

Suddenly Jack began to worry. Was he ready to play baseball after being on the trail for so long? What if he'd forgotten how? "I got a great idea, Billy. Let's go play some ball. Me and you. Just the two of us."

Billy took a long draw on his bottle of sweet tonic. "I ain't no ballplayer."

"You don't have to be. I just need to toss a ball around before tryouts tomorrow or I'll make a fool out of myself."

"What makes you think you won't anyhow?"

"I'm going to pretend you didn't say that, because, tell you what, Bill Henry. I believe you could be a top-notch ballplayer yourself." He stabbed the air with his fork as he spoke. "You have the eyes, the speed, fast, sure hands. All you need to do is learn the fundamentals."

"How long would that take?"

"Normally, about ten years or so. But lucky for you, you're not normal."

"Thank you." He loaded his *tortilla* with more meat. "What're you getting at?"

"What I mean is, if I just had a week or so, I believe I could turn you into a baseball man to be reckoned with."

"But you don't. And neither do I."

"Won't you just play toss with me? Just for a little while? I really need to get the rust off. Look, we'll go to the ball field, throw the ball around some, and that'll be it."

Billy said nothing else as his eyes once again roamed the cantina. He seemed to settle on someone, and when Jack turned to look, whom should he see but Mr. Becket approaching.

"Hello, lads," the old-timer said. Then he focused on Jack. "I trust you had a nice little chat with your uncle."

"Yes, sir. And I thank you for putting in a good word for me."

"Not at all. I wish him well. Come Sunday, he'll be facing a ruthless organization, and he's already short on men."

Billy took the cue. "Jack here figures on lending a hand. He's one of the best around."

Mr. Becket shared a smile with Billy. "So I've been told."

"What do you mean, a ruthless organization?" asked Jack. "Long John—I mean, *Uncle* John—he said something about that."

"Let's just say Mr. Hulbert of Chicago and your uncle do not share the same vision of the future of baseball. Aye, one is in it for the love of the game and the men who play it, the other for the money."

"Why do you say that?"

"Well, for one thing, Mr. Hulbert has begun to *reserve* the services of a ballplayer from year to year. That means the ball man must sign a contract agreeing to play for the same team next year for the same amount of money, or he doesn't play anywhere at all. Unless the owner releases him from his contract."

"That's not fair," said Jack.

"Aye, and John Dillon agrees. But I've told him it's one way to keep a team's payroll down—with so many teams folding lately due to finances."

Mr. Becket waved to Tia Rosa, who was setting a basket of sweet breads at a table she'd just cleared. "Better go grab my sweet breads, lads." He winked. "'Tis what I've been waiting for. Good dough. So rich and buttery."

Billy nodded.

Mr. Becket tipped his hat. "Gentlemen." He strolled away.

No one talked much after that as they both focused on cleaning their plates. But as soon as their boots hit the boardwalk outside, Billy slipped his arm around Jack's shoulder and said, "Okay, buddy. Let's go toss a ball."

"Really?" Jack stopped. "Just like that?"

"Look, don't jump to any conclusions. I'm just thinking that the ball field might be a good place to be while that marshal's still in town. That's all there is to it, all right?"

"Sure, Bill Henry, sure! Wait right here. I need to get my baseball. Oh, and I need a bat. They're in the stable."

"A bat? Hold on. To toss a ball?"

"Yeah. No, you'll see. Be right back." Jack ran full speed to the horse barn. He not only needed the bat and ball, he needed a favor.

From Eliza.

She was not alone when he arrived. Standing alongside Eliza as she balanced on a wooden crate grooming Homer was a strong young fellow. Jack quickly recognized him as the Dillontown second baseman, Jésus de Luz, who was in soft conversation with her.

Was Jésus sweet on her? Jack wondered.

Well, so what? Why should he care? Jack knew he had no time for a sidetrack into romance, not with all he had to accomplish.

So after a short pause and a deep breath at the barn door to regain his balance, Jack rolled right in, cool as a mountain stream.

"Hola, señorita," he said, using Spanish he had learned on the trail.

Both she and Jésus turned toward Jack.

"Hola," she said, smiling. "Jésus, this is the boy I was speaking about."

Jésus de Luz squared his broad shoulders at Jack and eyed him sternly. "This tall skinny boy?" he said. "You think he is good in *béisbol*?"

She does? thought Jack. My gosh! The girl was not only pretty, she was a fine judge of talent to boot. He stood taller.

Eliza turned back to Homer to continue running the curry brush over his back. Homer's coat gleamed with her handiwork.

"And who are you to talk, Jésus?" she said. "*See-row*-for-four today, at the bat, *que incluye* a rolling ball back to the pitcher and a pop-up fly *heet* to the shortstop?"

Jésus did not try to defend himself. He strode toward Jack. "Eliza, she tells me you are John Dillon's nephew."

"Well, yes, sir," said Jack, extending his hand and his chest. "I'm Jack Dillon. And I saw you play today and I think you are one amazing ball man. I surely do."

Jésus did not bother shaking Jack's hand. Through a smirk, he said, "That is true, skinny boy. And I respect your uncle. But he has earned it."

With that he brushed past Jack toward the open doorway, then turned, calling back to him. "You are leaving? *Sí*?"

"Uh, *sí*," said Jack. "Just stopped by to pick up my bat and ball."

"Then you hurry." He left.

"Oh, don't listen to him," said Eliza. "He has a bad mood. The team, they are all worried."

"Well, he shouldn't take it out on me. I'm here to save the day." He repuffed his chest.

She laughed. "You are funny. I told him your plan to help the team. *Ay, pero,* he is not so sure. You are, he is right, a little *es-kinny*."

"Skinny? Well, I'm still growing. I'm only—oh, never mind.

Eliza, right now, my partner out there"—Jack tipped his hat toward the street—"Bill Henry, and I, being two top-o'-the-rack crackerjack baseballists—we're heading down to the ball field to loosen up so's we can be in tiptop shape for the tryout tomorrow."

"Ah, *está bien*," she said. "I am glad."

"Yes, well . . ." Jack stepped closer, standing eye to eye with Eliza, who was still atop the apple crate. "I need your help with a secret baseball idea I've been tossing around. But this secret is so amazing it will barn-stoggle your mind."

"A secret." She lowered her voice. "Of course."

"I need another bat."

"I will never tell a soul." She made the sign of the cross.

"No, no. That's not the secret. I just really do need an extra bat."

She drew back her head, grinning. "Oh, my brother, he has many."

"Your brother?"

"Sí, Jésus."

"Ah, Jésus. He's your *brother*. Excellent." Jack leaned even closer. "All right, then. Here's my secret plan, and I'd like you to help me, *por favor*."

She was all eyes.

At the field, it took no time for Jack to see that Billy was more of an athlete than he'd imagined. Billy tossed the ball and caught it barehanded with comfort and ease, nonchalantly throwing it back while gazing off somewhere in the distance as if he'd done this sort of thing all his life.

After each catch, Jack brought the old baseball up near his nose and breathed in the musky smell of the soft deerskin leather, stuffed with acorns and clay, wrapped in yarn and stitched with yucca twine. There were better balls these days, but this one, from the mountains of New Mexico, he had made himself.

He loved the smell and the feel. To catch it. Then to throw it, to send it flying off his fingers with a snap of the wrist and watch it sail.

After one last toss, Jack walked up to Billy in the middle of the infield, gripping the bat Eliza had lent him. "All right. Here's my idea. You stand right here, and I'm going to hit the ball to you."

"To *me*?" Billy shook his head. "Son, son, son."

"Come on, Billy. Just try it. What do you have to lose? Besides, it's my grand idea."

"Oh, it is? Twenty feet away? Aren't we a little close?"

"No, no, I have a special way of hitting. And you'll be amazed at what a great baseball man you'll become after only one time playing this game."

Billy seemed to be considering the idea. "Have you tried it before?"

"Well, now." Jack's voice squeaked, and he fought the fiercest urge to cough into his hand. "Well, okay. Fair question. Uh, not entirely."

"Not at all?"

"That's another way of putting it."

Billy threw his hat at Jack, who ducked just in time.

Retrieving the hat, Jack ran back to Billy, trying to cook up another idea. But Billy beat him to it. "Why don't you ask *her*? I bet she'd play."

Jack looked toward the dugout near third base. Forgetting that he had invited her out, he now needed to show—as any good scout would—that he knew she'd been there all along. "Her? Oh, I thought about it, but I just decided that won't work."

"*¿Qué?*" said Eliza indignantly. She placed both hands on her hips. That's when Jack noticed she was wearing a blacksmith's glove on one hand. That is, the remnants of a blacksmith's glove. The cuff had been trimmed off, and all the fingers were cut away. She had come to play.

Slapping a fist into the palm of her glove, she said simply, "I have four brothers."

Jack did not return her fire. "I didn't say you couldn't play."

"*Sí, pero,* I see the look."

Jack winced and turned away. "Billy, what do you say now? If she can, then you can. And with two, this game'll be even better. Come on."

Billy shrugged and even showed a small grin. "Only because you're letting her," he said. Soon he was lined up near the pitcher's box, a few feet from Eliza, as Jack had instructed them to do.

At home base with the bat on his shoulder, Jack held up the ball. "Ready?"

104

Eliza leaned over and placed her hands on her knees. *"Heet* the ball," she growled.

Billy copied her stance and her voice. "Yeah, you clown. *Heet* it."

Jack flipped the ball up and knocked a grounder toward Billy, who latched onto it with both hands. "Now what?"

"Pitch it back to me."

Billy drew his arm behind him in an underhand motion. "Where do you want it?"

Jack held his bat level, waist high. "Right here. But throw the ball from your shoulder. That's how they're tossing it these days."

Billy flung the deerskin ball, and Jack struck it, this time sending a bouncer to Eliza. She took a step back, but still managed to slap her leather palm around the ball and snug it close.

"Same thing, *por favor,*" said Jack.

Eliza obliged, with a throw that was wide but close enough. And the game was on. Back and forth went the ball, and no matter where the fielders placed it, Jack managed to swing and sock it back to them in perfect order. Billy, then Eliza, then Billy again. It soon became automatic, fluid, almost like a dance.

"From where did you learn this game?" asked Eliza. "I like it."

"It came to me in a dream." Jack swatted another. "I call it 'chili pepper.'"

"You dream this?" she asked.

"Sure. I do that all the time." To be accurate, his father had shown him something similar. But on the trail one night in New

Mexico, drifting off to sleep, Jack had imagined playing with his father an even faster version of chili pepper, in the form he was showing them today.

After a while, Eliza said, "I want to try."

Jack caught the ball and smiled at her. "Well, now. I know I might make it look easy, Eliza. But the truth is . . ."

"The truth is, get out here," said Billy. "Let her try it."

Two against one, thought Jack. Great. He tromped out and joined Billy in the field, casually tugging the girl's glove onto his left hand—just to see what it was like.

Eliza stepped up to bat.

After a few pitches, however, Jack felt slightly redeemed. What may have seemed so simple—and had likely looked even simpler—was somewhat of a challenge for Eliza. Slowly, though, over time, she began to get the hang of the technique. It was plain to see there were athletes in her family as well.

But Billy was his official student. So when Billy finally stepped up to bat, Jack was ready with some official advice. "Show patience," he said. "Choke up and wait until the ball is just about on you."

"Choke up?"

"Slide your hands up the handle a few inches."

He did. "Like this?"

"That's perfect. Then angle the bat so it bounces the ball right where you want it to go and just punch it."

The results astounded Jack. Billy was both a great observer and a fast learner. How else to explain his immediate ease and command of the game?

Within minutes, Billy had become so good, he was already tapping, swatting, whacking, and adjusting to throws high or low or hard to reach.

Eliza said it first, but only because Jack could scarcely believe what he was seeing. "You are natural at this, Billy."

"See, Billy?" said Jack. "That's why you should learn baseball. You *are* a natural."

Jack got no argument from this nimble desperado with a gun on his hip, this Lincoln County soldier who had, as legends told, shot his way into and out of countless do-or-die situations across the western plains. But even he was now being held captive by the innocent game of baseball.

At sunset when they called it quits, Billy offered, "Maybe tomorrow, we'll play some more."

Hearing that thrilled Jack. Now he had two pals to practice with and someone to help him teach Billy as well.

After promising to be back in the morning, Eliza ran off, her long braid flying. Watching her, Billy said, "She likes you."

"Me? She likes baseball, that's all."

"Don't tell me you didn't see it."

"See what?" Jack studied the empty path Eliza had just traveled, as if it might hold a clue. "I mean, sure I saw it—whatever it was." He squinted harder.

Billy swung his head low. "Son, how much do you know about girls?"

"Girls?" Jack folded his arms. "Shoot, I know just about all there is to—well, I mean, I know all I'll ever need to know, that's for sure."

Billy pursed his lips in pity. "Sorry to say, son, but no man on earth will ever gain anywhere near that much knowledge. Life ain't long enough, and girls are just fiercely complex."

He slung his arm over Jack. "Look, it's been a big day. I found us a new camp, closer in, on the edge of town. What say let's go?"

Slowly, the two tired ballplayers started off toward the hills, toward certainty and away from complexity, away from the perplexing unknowns.

"Billy?" Jack ventured. "You think you could teach me about girls?"

Billy exhaled loudly. Twice. Then he said, "Son, I just taught you everything I know."

That night, sipping coffee around the campfire, a curiosity gripped Jack about this man who now seemed as close to him as his own brother had once been. There was one question that had been sitting in Jack's mind since the very first night, and he decided that now was the time to ask it.

"What's it like, Billy, being Billy the Kid and all?"

The outlaw glanced at Jack over the flicker of flame, then tossed the dregs of his coffee away. "It ain't what you think. I tell you, there's more truth in the dime-store novels I got stashed in my travel bag than in all the newspaper reports about Billy the Kid."

Jack held Billy's gaze a moment, unconvinced. "How so?"

Billy rose. He took a short branch and stirred the fire, knocking down the flames and bringing the coals to bright embers. "Because I am Billy. I'm just not Billy the Kid."

"I don't get it."

An irritation rose in his voice. "I'm not the man they make me out to be, all right?" Billy scratched the coals once more, then flung the stick at them and sat back down. "I'm just an accidental outlaw, for the most part, plain and simple."

"You're saying it was all an accident? That what happened to you was just by chance? I mean, did you kill all those men or not?"

"How many do you think it's been?"

"Twenty or thirty, according to the newspapers."

"Newspapers lie, son. They're as bad as the government. Truth is, I've been in spots where I've had to fight for my life. Back in Lincoln County, I was in a war."

"I know. I heard about that."

Billy grunted. "I can imagine what you heard. But I never did anything a soldier wouldn't have done. I was hired on to help a good man get out of a fix that was not his fault. And if I fired my gun, then I was in a spot where it was either kill or be killed."

"You never shot that deputy in cold blood?"

"I shot a man I wished I didn't have to. But my life was at stake."

"So you're just saying, the truth has yet to be told?"

"I suppose. But what I'm really saying is, at this point, I have no confidence it ever will be."

"So you can't really shoot a coin out of the sky?"

"'Course I can. But that's not the truth I mean."

Billy stretched out to gain a bit more comfort on his bedroll. "I never asked for this life, believe me. At fourteen, I was orphaned, just like you. And I needed to provide for myself. One day, I hired on at a lumber camp in the hills of New Mexico, where there happened to be a bully of a man, name of Cahill, who got a thrill out of beating on me. So I saved up, bought a gun, and learned to use it."

"So, you just—I mean, what happened?"

"Next time we crossed tracks, Cahill, this grown man, started in on thrashing me again. Pinning me down with his knees and beating me. And when he wouldn't stop, I finally worked my arm free and shot him. Self-defense, as I saw it. But with the friends he had in that town, I would've hung. So I hit the trail. And I've been on the dodge ever since."

"Why don't you just quit? Just hang up your guns?"

"Not that easy. But I do give it thought. One reason I came to California. To see if one day, down the line . . ." He drifted.

"Really? So you might? You might just flat give up outlawing?"

"Who knows? But if I were to, a town like this would be better'n most. People coming and going all the time. Miners, cowboys, gamblers. They're all keep-to-'emselves types of people. Lets a man feel free to be himself."

"So that's what you meant—hiding in plain sight."

Billy pulled one knee up against his chest. "Yep, pretty much. I always thought if I ever found the right place, I'd head back to New Mexico and bring my girl out. Settle down, change my name—shoot, I've done that a few times. And start all over again new."

"But what about all the lawmen, the bounty hunters, all of them out to get you and claim that reward?"

"You know, son, I've come to see that there is little difference between the men on one side of the law and those on the other. Ruthless killers as well as good men can be found on both sides. So I'd just have to be on my toes. Just like a ballplayer, right?"

This was better news than Jack could even say. There was a real chance that this man known the world 'round might up and decide to stay right here, in Jack's new town, fit in, and maybe even play ball.

"What's her name?" asked Jack. "Your girl."

"Paulita." Billy's eyes wandered the fire a moment. "Paulita Maxwell. Lives outside Fort Sumner. I cowboyed for her father, Pedro, a while. She's a sweet gal."

Jack let the nervous coals take over for a long while, jittering, turning orange and blue depending upon how the breeze trickled over them. It was a lot for him to take in, to realize that there could be such a thing as an accidental outlaw—because of circumstances—that other men could force you into a life you did not choose, but one which you could not avoid.

As the coals settled, Jack determined that he would never do such a thing. Whatever life was ahead of him, Jack decided, it would be of his own choosing. Any other type of life, he'd be sure to avoid.

Especially if it meant he'd have to kill or be killed.

With a quick jolt, Billy rose from his sleeping roll to one knee, his gun drawn. Whispering over the fire, he said, "Someone's here."

Jack hunched low, not knowing what else to do.

The coals lit Billy's face like an orange ghost. He cocked the hammer on his pistol and spun toward the dense brush.

Who's there?" said Billy. *"¿Quién es?"*

"Un amigo," said a voice. "I have no gun."

Out of the brush, a big man appeared. As the light hit him, Jack saw right away that it was the catcher for the Dillontown Nine. Young, about Billy's age, dark, he wore a black cowboy shirt and a brown felt hat. From the crown of the hat, a long reddish-brown feather protruded out of a snakeskin band.

"My name is Blackjack Buck," he said. "And I have a message for you."

Billy lowered his gun. "Sorry, my friend. We weren't expecting any company." He waved the man closer. "Come, have a seat."

"What's the message?" asked Jack.

The big catcher glanced his way, then crouched toward the ground, saying nothing. Steadying himself, he looked around the camp. "Do you have anything to drink—besides the coffee?"

"Sorry," said Billy. "Don't believe neither one of us drinks spirits."

"Then," said the visitor, "I will be forced to dip into my own." He pulled out a thin glass flask from inside his shirt, uncorked it, and took a gulp.

"Ah," he said, savoring the black liquid. "This I must do. The pain, *es grande*."

"Sorry to hear that," said Billy.

Blackjack Buck shrugged. "The *padres* at the church, they make this tonic for me. Cactus applejack and blackberry wine."

After a moment, he lowered his head and closed his eyes. In a low, strong voice, he began to speak.

Blackjack Buck's in a wine barrel room
A barrelhouse king who sees all things.

From the mouth of Chaco Canyon
to the mountains of the moon,
comes a boy on the winds of the elderberry flute
to the drums of the boom-lay boom.

I see him ride to battle
to face the evils of a rat.
In his rifle scabbard laced low and tight,
I see a baseball bat.

When the man fell silent, Jack leaned forward, whispering. "Well, doggone. I keep a baseball bat in my saddle. I think that one verse is about me." He turned to Billy to gain support. "Could be, right, Billy?"

Billy looked at Blackjack Buck. "Is that what it means, Señor Buck? This boy's riding to battle?"

"It means what it says," the prophet answered, his eyes still shut.

That did not satisfy Billy. "But Chaco Canyon. That's in New Mexico. Navajo country. I've been there. You talking about me?"

"But I have, too," said Jack. "I think that's where I made my baseball."

Billy ignored the comment. "Who's the rat, *amigo*? You don't say that."

"There is still more."

The prophet continued.

I see rich men and lawmen in cahoots
'Gainst men borne of baseball blood.
I see the holy game wrapped in chains
Till freed by a hundred-year flood.

Blackjack Buck opened his eyes, as if from a deep sleep, and looked straight ahead.

"Well, now," said Billy. "What should we make of that?"

"Last week," said the prophet, "I saw both of you play the game of chili pepper."

"Last week?" said Jack, somehow feeling relief at the man's mistake. "But we never met up until yesterday. And we never played the game before today."

"In a dream."

"Oh."

"In the dream, there is a fancy white man in a white coat

watching everything you do. This man, he has the eyes of a desert rat." Pointing to his own eyes, the visionary exclaimed, *"¡Los ojos de la rata!* So I have come to give you a warning. Stay apart from this man."

"Any particular reason?" asked Billy.

"Sí. He has a bullet for one of you."

Jack lurched forward. "Which one of us?"

The prophet shrugged again. "Nothing more is clear. Both of you are in my vision. I see a gun. I hear a blast." He turned his palms up.

Billy folded his arms. "Well, we'll keep an eye out for rats, *amigo.* We appreciate the warning." He grinned, looking now at Jack. "What else can we do?"

Jack only stared back at him. If Billy didn't know, he sure didn't.

The prophet rose to his full height. "Tomorrow morning, you must meet me at the field of *béisbol.* Both of you. We will play the game of chili pepper. It is good for the eyes, for locking the eyes. This you must do before presenting yourselves to the eyes of John Dillon."

Jack brought up a knee and rested his elbow on it. "So you know why I'm here? I mean, I guess you would, now, wouldn't you?"

"I know why both of you are here."

Billy shot a glance, his eyes fixed on the visionary.

"Do not worry," said Blackjack Buck, returning the gaze. "Your secret is safe with me."

As suddenly as their guest had appeared, he was gone.

There is nothing so magical as that moment during the battle of a game when a batsman first realizes his eyes are locked in. It is an occurrence so rare, so fleeting, that we forever remember if it has ever happened to us or if we have ever seen it take place within the soul of another.

It begins without notice. Then from at bat to at bat, the baseball striker feels a brace of confidence building. After a game or two, he realizes he is locking in to the delivery, speed, and trajectory of every pitch thrown his way.

"I'm seeing the ball," he says, and that is all he says. For he and his benchmates know it is not a thing to be discussed.

To be locked in, locked on, to stand at bat with the hunter's eye and steady calm, trigger-ready, to strike the ball hard every time, sending it screaming off across the grass or out into the ether, is equal to seeing a meteor streak through the sky and land nearby. It is the first kiss, the first secret glimpse of the girl you will marry. It is a lucky thing. A fleeting thing.

It is rarely, though, a repeatable thing. And as quickly as it arrives, it will depart, both moments cloaked in the mysteries of grace.

Ah, but thus it is with all such gifts in life, like good luck or unearned love, which only angels can arrange.

"Awake, you snake!" said Billy, shaking Jack out of a deep sleep. "Day's a-breakin'. Coffee's in the pot, hotcakes a-bakin'!"

"Hotcakes?" said Jack, blinking. "Really?"

"Well, sort of. Wish I had some eggs to fluff 'em up." He held out a flat piece of cooked dough and flapped it around.

"How long you been up?"

"Crack of dawn, son." Billy stood tall, waving his arm. "Lookin' at the beauty of this land. Mountains, trees, wildflowers, sagebrush, streams. Probably saw a dozen deer in the meadow. Sure ain't Lincoln County."

"Yep." Jack stretched against his bedding and yawned at the sky. "These are some big mountains."

"I've already been up the ridge, looking around."

"What?" Jack rolled to his side. "I'm your scout, Billy. You gotta wait for me."

"You're sleeping like a baby over there. I can't wait till noon."

Jack bolted up. "What time is it? It ain't noon."

"Pretty close. I'd say it's past seven."

Jack lowered himself back down. "Where I come from, *son*, that ain't noon." He squinted at the sunlight streaming through the sparse branches of a scrub oak tree. "I couldn't sleep a wink last night, Billy, being so wound up."

"You were sleeping just then."

"At long last maybe." He turned around and shook out his hat, which he'd used as a pillow. He punched the dome with his fist, still feeling awestruck by the crisp bullet holes in the six-inch crown. "I wanted to be up and on down to the ball field by now."

"Relax. Grab some coffee and grub."

Jack glanced over at a stack of burnt dough cakes, still smoking in a black pan sitting on a rock.

"Billy?" he began, yanking his derby tight. "You know all that gold you won playing poker? Why don't we go into town and have us a café breakfast? Or at least we could stock up on some real food."

"Maybe later. One thing I learned over the years, my boy, is to preserve what you have as long as you can. Reason is, you never know when'll be the next time you're down to nothing."

"I didn't mean squander it. Just get us a fried egg or two. Like you said. Or at least a little honey for these"—he paused to reconsider the smoking stack—"hotcakes."

"As I say, maybe later. But I am sort of anxious to get to town and hear what more Señor Buck might've dreamed up regarding our predicament."

"You believe in prophecy?"

"No, I don't, to be honest. That's not what caught my attention. However, any man who knows my secrets is a man I'd like to keep close by. At least until I learn what he knows."

"Like me, Billy?"

That seemed to catch the outlaw by surprise. "You, son? Well,

I keep you in close range because I figure that's just one more crazy desperado I won't have to tangle with out on the range. Now, get up."

When Jack and Billy arrived at the ball field later that morning, they found Blackjack Buck standing near the home stone with a bat on his shoulder.

"Buenos dias," he called.

"Buenos dias," said Billy. "How'd you sleep?"

"I do not remember. But it happens to me a lot."

"What do you remember?" asked Jack, eager to learn more about the cryptic prophecy. "Did you have another dream?"

The prophet tapped the bat on the ground. "Gentlemen, I have seen nothing new. Shall we begin?"

"Might as well," said Billy.

"Está bien. Go back to the pitcher's box. Line up about six feet apart." Those instructions sounded familiar, thought Jack. Still, he jumped to it.

Blackjack Buck took a batter's stance. *"¿Listos?"* Without waiting for a response, he cracked a sharp one-hopper to Billy.

He grabbed it wordlessly and tossed it back, and the prophet began stroking the ball with precision. From Jack to Billy, then Jack again. Billy did not remove his gun, but even with the leather holster slapping his hip, he moved like a deer. He had actually improved over yesterday. What's going on? Jack wondered. How did Billy, all of a sudden, became a ballist of great skill?

For ten minutes, twenty, half an hour, they played chili pepper. The Dillontown catcher rapped balls across the ground, little drives straight to the fielders, and even some one-hop bouncers high into the sky.

Then Jack stepped up to bat. And it was the same for him. Every ball he hit was sharp and nearly to the exact spot he'd intended. Overnight, his skill had doubled, too.

Billy at first refused to take his turn at bat. "I'm happy just doing this."

"It is not enough," said Blackjack Buck.

And Jack wouldn't let him get out of it, either—especially if he was declining only because Jack had just shown him up. "Drop that gun belt and play. Come on. You know you should."

Apparently deciding not to cause a stir of any sort, Billy motioned surrender with an open palm and stepped up. And he continued to shine. He hit everything.

A few poor tosses didn't matter. Lightning reflexes made up for any stray pitch as he scrambled to rap every one with snap and ginger, moving the bat around as if it were a sword. He showed far more skill than Jack.

At first it bothered him, seeing how easily things came to Billy, until Jack noticed that Billy was locked on. It was something he had seen only a handful of times before. Fully focused, with a confidence approaching arrogance and with athletic grace, Billy struck any pitch that came his way. It was a display no true ballist could ever envy or begrudge. Certainly not Jack. It would be akin to an artist resenting a rainbow.

During the intense, fast-paced game, several townsfolk, including Eliza, had gathered around the field to watch. A few of the Dillontown Nine had even wandered up, ahead of the tryouts, and they were struck with what they saw as well.

"Quite a show I'm seeing, Bill Henry," called Fence Post Hayes after the game ended. "You're as quick at hitting as you are at sweeping winnings off the poker table."

Billy barely acknowledged the compliment, wiping sweat from his forehead with his shirtsleeve, almost as if he were hiding behind his arm.

The prophet was more explicit. "You are quick and solid," he said. "It is as if you know this game from deep in your spirit."

That observation made Billy finally admit to playing a similar game of stick and ball as a little tyke in New York City. But he deflected the praise. "Shoot, I haven't touched a baseball in years. I just like the challenge of it. Fun to see what I can do."

The other ballplayers wandered onto the field with the same general comments. As they did, Billy retreated more and more, finally giving Jack a backhanded slap on the shoulder. "I'm goin' to the saloon." He started off.

"What? Wait." Jack ran to catch up. "Billy, you can't leave now. The tryout's about to begin."

Billy kept walking, motioning for Jack to follow. They strode down the tiered wood steps of the first-base dugout for privacy.

"That was a mistake," said Billy. "I didn't come here to stand out. I came here to blend in."

"But don't you see? You will blend in. You are a true ballplayer in a town full of ballplayers."

"No, no. They recognized me. Several of these men. I could feel it in their stares. Next thing you know, the marshal will be down here all over me."

Turning around and scanning the grounds to make certain no one was paying them any mind, Jack said, "Wait, now, wait. Doggone it. Is that what you felt? Because I felt something else. They were watching you, sure, but they didn't see the Kid. They saw a baseball man putting on a show—something you just don't see every day."

Billy took in a slow breath and let it out. "Well, then, once again, folks have misidentified me and built me into something I'm not." He climbed the steps. "I'm going to play some cards, son. I also hope to inquire about land."

"You do? So soon? I mean, I'm your scout. That's what I'm gettin' paid to do."

Billy could not stop a smile. "Some scout you are. You let a fellow sneak up on our camp last night. Then you sleep till all hours and bellyache about the grub. Then you come here and let half the town creep up on me while I'm fixed on playing a child's game." He reached out and yanked Jack's hat down over his eyes.

"Doggone it, Billy. I'm still gettin' used to the job." Jack pulled his hat up just in time to see the plump little man in the white suit come charging from across the field, heading right up to them. As he approached, the man squinted at Billy with small yellowy eyes—like a rat.

Now Jack knew exactly who he was.

With his hand outstretched, the man called to Billy. "Pleased to meet you, son. Vernon Toots is the name, and have I got the perfect ball club for you. Yes, sir. They arrive tomorrow. Number one team in the land."

He sent Billy a wormy grin.

Billy did not take the Rat Man's hand.

It didn't matter much, since Fence Post rushed up, grabbed the rotund fellow by the shoulder, and spun him around.

"Now, just a flea-flickin' minute," he bellowed. "You can't just do-si-do in here and snatch up one of our ballplayers."

"Excuse me, but I don't believe he has signed a contract with anyone."

"Not yet. He just arrived. But—"

The man interrupted him. "But, you're not prepared to offer him what I am—to play for the world-famous Chicago White Stockings." He cast a glance at Billy. "For a bundle of money."

As Billy tried to back away, Jack shuffled over and blocked him again, urging him to stay with his eyes. Billy obliged with a weary shake of his head, probably worried Jack would make a scene.

"For money?" Fence Post looked around at the other ballplayers bunched up behind him. They all nodded. He turned back to Mr. Toots. "We are willing to beat any offer you have in mind."

"One hundred dollars for a one-day contract?" The Rat Man smiled.

Even Billy was impressed, pulling in a quick breath.

Fence Post lifted his hat and scratched his bald head.

Mr. Toots read the reaction. "I thought not."

Fence Post growled at the Chicagoan. "Then you thought wrong, you fat-faced city-bred toad sucker. *Two* hundred dollars, gold, is our offer, and if you interfere once more, you're going to be watching the game tomorrow from Last Out Hill."

All the men rumbled in agreement. The Dillontown cemetery, apparently, had a limited view of the ball field.

"Can I say something here?" asked Billy, who did not wait for an answer. "Gentlemen, I am flattered by your interest." He motioned toward Jack. "But this here's the boy you want. He's taught me everything I know about baseball."

Blackjack Buck stepped forward. *"Amigo,"* he said to Billy. "You *and* this boy will join our team. I have seen it."

Jack stared hard at the prophet. Could this be true?

"And that settles it," Fence Post announced, placing his arm on Billy's shoulder, telling him, "If you've been away from the game as long as you say, and you still play as cat-quick with hand, foot, and stick as you just showed, by golly, ain't no telling what you might do, once you work the rust off."

The folks nearby offered loud murmurs of accord.

Vernon Toots shook a chubby fist as he stood back, focusing his beady eyes on Billy. "If you play for Dillontown, my boy, you are making a grave mistake, mark my words. And I mean a *grave* mistake."

Fence Post jumped in again. "Shut your smokin' pipe hole, little fella. The only mistake he's makin' is not pounding you into the ground with a fence post. But me, I ain't so polite."

126

Like the mind reader he likely was, Blackjack Buck walked up with Fence Post's trusty "bat" and presented it to him.

Vernon Toots did not wait around for any posthole ground-pounding. He skipped out of there like a two-legged lizard scampering through campfire coals.

Smiling, Jack spun back toward Billy. "See here, Bill Henry? You're gonna fit right in!" Before Billy could muster a reply, a booming voice roared from across the field.

"Gentlemen, gather 'round." Long John Dillon, wearing a black ball cap and black baseball leggings, had finally rolled onto the ball field. "If you are here for the tryout, come forward."

A bunch of hopeful men hurried toward the big man. Several Dillontowners scattered bats and balls across the infield to help with the setup.

"All right, now," called John Dillon. "I don't have all day." He paused to count the hopefuls and jot down their names.

Approaching Jack, he said, "Son, I cannot play favorites. And I don't want you wasting my time."

"No, sir. I understand. I won't."

The cap'n turned and huddled with Blackjack Buck a moment, then again addressed the gathering. "Seven men gather at the home stone. Grab one of those bats and spread wide of each other. You other seven, gather around the pitcher's box, pick up a ball, and face off with one of the men holding a bat."

Everyone hustled to one spot or another. Jack and Billy paired up together, with Billy batting first.

"Good enough," said John Dillon as he stepped toward the backstop. "Hitters, get ready to hit. Pitchers, you will pitch. But be ready to field any ball that comes your way—and you may see more'n one. I am looking for all-around finesse, skill, dexterity, and reflexes in a high-pressure situation."

This is very strange, thought Jack. But Long John Dillon's the expert. I'll just do what he says and hope for the best.

From behind the batters, Uncle John lifted his cap. "When I drop my hat, gentlemen, make your pitch."

The hat dropped. Jack licked his fingers.

Six pitchers threw their pitches, sidearm style. After a pause, Jack tossed his with the overhand thrust they had used in chili-pepper practice. The scene was a genuine mess. One batter was hit by a neighboring pitcher. One pitcher nearly got beaned by a wayward shot. Billy had actually swung at and hit two pitches in quick succession, one out of self-defense. But the other one he hit—Jack's pitch—made everyone's jaw drop. That ball sailed high over the head of Blackjack Buck, who was now standing out in center field.

Long John Dillon simply watched the ball, making no comment other than to bark, "Pitchers, step up, take a bat, and prepare to hack. Batters, chase your baseballs as fast as you can. I'm looking for speed. Then come back and pitch."

Everyone scrambled. Billy had the farthest to run, but he was back in no time. "Where do you want it?" he asked.

Jack held his bat belt high. "Right here, *amigo.*"

Billy served up a perfect pitch and Jack sent it sky high, straight out to left field. A grand shot. The recent practicing had paid off for him, too.

A couple more times through, and in ten minutes, it was all over.

"I've seen enough!" John Dillon declared. "Thank you, gentlemen, for your participation."

During the tryouts—the most bizarre Jack had ever seen—Long John Dillon had certainly treated everyone equally. Each man—and boy—was questioned about position and experience. Each received a chance to hit, run, field, and throw under pressure and scrutiny. Just like in a real game. But how in the world could a proper assessment of skills be made in ten minutes? Still, Jack's hopes were high.

After talking a moment with Blackjack Buck, Long John stepped toward the group of winded ballists. He held a sheet of paper in his hand. "Gentlemen, we thank you all for showing up and doing your best. I will call out two names. If you hear your name, please come forward. If not, I thank you again for your interest."

Everyone seemed to take a breath along with Cap'n Dillon, who then announced, "Jim Buckles and Tom LaFay."

The two men bolted forth with loud whoops.

Jack looked at Billy with shock. "I don't understand. Those two are not close to being the players we are."

"I don't quite understand either," said Billy. "I thought at least one of us would be chosen."

Long John Dillon strode up to Buckles and LaFay. "Congratulations, men. Buckles, I like your bat. LaFay, you are an extraordinary infielder. Be sure to come to my saloon when that stage pulls in later today. We'll set you boys up with everything you need."

Billy shrugged. "Well, doesn't hurt my feelings any." He flipped the ball to Jack. "Sorry, son, but as they say in baseball, I gotta go."

"No one says that."

Then, as if dancing across a ballroom floor, Long John Dillon sidestepped right over to Jack and Billy. "You two," he said. "A moment, please."

"Yes, sir," said Billy.

"I judge you boys to be fair competitors with some genuine skill for the game. But I also judge you as being just too young and unschooled to hold your own on a field of well-experienced men in a crucial game. I do believe, however, that you would benefit from witnessing this game sitting alongside me and the other boys. But that's it. If you agree, you will each sign a one-day contract, but do not expect to play. Is that agreeable?"

"A contract?" said Jack. "You mean it?"

The cap'n laughed. "Well, I understand I already got roped into writing one for Bill here by that Toots fellow. So I might as well include you."

"Fine with me," said Billy, as if anyone could turn down money like that.

"Fine with me, too!" cried Jack, who cared nothing about money. He immediately tilted back his head, spun in a circle in the middle of the field, and gazed into the clouds.

This was the best news ever. For he knew nothing was going to stop him from playing now.

They're here! They're here!" Several young boys, yelling in glee, pointed down the street toward the high mountain road leading into town. "The Chicago White Stockings are here!"

Out in the distance, Jack could see three red stagecoaches with four horses each, kicking up dust. Men fired their guns throughout the town as boys and girls raised their voices in jubilee, running off toward the parade of coaches. Soon they came rolling down Maine Street, with children running alongside and men and women cheering them on. Slowing to a trot, the horses pulled up in front of Coleman's 4-Bagger Hotel.

"Want to go see them?" Jack asked Billy.

"Suppose I might. Pulling up next to a poker game, aren't they?"

It seemed the entire town had sprung into action. Out of the hotel emerged a five-piece brass band of trombones and trumpets, followed by three drummer boys, and they were all playing a raucous tune that occasionally resembled "Turkey in the Straw."

By the time Jack and Billy drew close, each Chicago ballist

had disembarked into the throng carrying a satchel upon which the player had his name engraved in silver. All of a sudden, as if in a dream, ball-yard heroes, with names from the *St. Louis Post and Dispatch* headlines, took on human form and were standing right there in front of Jack.

The band played on. This time the drummers shouted out some of the players' names in a song.

"King Kelly, Cap Anson," they sang. "George Gore, time for dancin'!"

Men and women locked arms and slide-stepped on the board-walk. Children skipped in rhythm. It was a carnival.

"Cap Anson," Jack heard himself say, reading the silver lettering on the man's leather case. "He is a living legend, Billy. Just like Uncle John, he plays first base and runs the team. And he's shrewd as can be."

Jack read another case. "There's Joe Quest! One of the finest second baggers around." He ran forward, turned, and beckoned Billy to come closer. "I want you to see these fellows."

"I can see."

The song went on. "Corcoran, Burns, Cal McVey, and Silver Flint are here today!" It was a tricky little tune, Jack thought, catchy and right clever.

"Yonder *is* Cal McVey," he shouted as he read that player's name. "First man ever to get six hits in one game, and he did it twice in the same week. And I see George Gore! He's a top-notch striker. He batted .360 last season."

Billy smiled. "You don't say."

"This is going to be the most fun I've ever had in my life. I never dreamed I would ever get to see—" Jack stopped as one particular player caught his eye. Dressed in flashy brown and yellow calico pants, a puffy white shirt, and a blue silk vest was Mike "King" Kelly, the grandest base stealer of all time, not to mention a .300 hitter.

"Mr. Kelly!" Jack ran up, unable to stop himself. "I am a big, big admirer of yours."

Mr. Kelly, appearing woozy from the trip, squinted sternly at Jack. "Are ye big enough to fetch me a bottla whiskey, lad, and a coupla cold beers?"

Before Jack could answer, three men nearby accepted the task.

"Some hero," said Billy, stepping close.

Jack was not dismayed. "He appears to be thirsty is all."

Leaving their travel grips on the boardwalk, the players did not enter the hotel. Instead, they were led next door into the Touch 'Em All by Long John Dillon, who ordered a tall glass of beer for each traveler. The crowd inside swelled, filling all ten or twelve tables and the standing room as well. Jack and Billy followed, settling themselves along the side wall of the saloon, just below a display of bull-horn skulls and six-foot-long rattle-snake skins. From that vantage point, Jack noticed, Billy could see the bar, the mirror above the bar, the foot of the fancy stairs, and the swinging double-door entry to the saloon. No one could come or go without him knowing.

The White Stockings grabbed chairs at the finely decorated oval tables in front. Draped in red tablecloths, they held half a dozen rabbit-skin pouches full of chewing tobacco, spread out, one in front of every chair. Once the guests began to partake of their beverages, a loud, sharp crack resounded from the varnished bar top and brought all talking to a halt. It was Long John Dillon, wielding a bat and calling for order. All eyes fixed on the dark, barrel-chested man.

"Ladies and gentlemen. As owner and manager of the Dillontown Nine, it is my pleasure to welcome from Chicago, Illinois, the champion Chicago White Stockings, and especially their proud owner, Mr. William Hulbert."

"Hear, hear," shouted the crowd, with beers aloft.

During the cheer, however, Jack noticed that two White Stocking players—Cap Anson and King Kelly—began speaking in harsh whispers between themselves. Were they arguing? What about? Mr. Anson's eyes glared strongly as he pointed toward the Dillontown cap'n and huffed out a harsh phrase to Kelly.

John Dillon did not seem to notice. The room fell quiet again. "I will now ask Mr. Hulbert to introduce each of the men on his great team before they head next door for some well-deserved rest."

Mr. Hulbert, the notorious coal baron, overdressed in a dark suit, vest, white shirt, and bow tie, stood and walked to the bar to stand alongside John Dillon. Rather a pale man with a dark mustache and trimmed beard, he proceeded to call out the names of each man on his twelve-man roster. One by one, they all stepped forward, wooden-faced, and gave a nod. Then Hulbert turned to Cap'n Dillon. "I have a strongbox containing ten thousand dollars in United States currency, and I wish to request a stakeholder."

"What's that?" Jack whispered.

Billy leaned close. "Someone to hold the prize each club is putting at stake."

The coal baron raised his voice. "The sheriff, perhaps. Or justice of the peace? Someone of authority."

No one stirred.

John Dillon cleared his throat. "Well, sir, we don't exactly have a sheriff nor a justice of any doggone peace. All we have in our town is an umpire. If there's a dispute between two parties, the proper way to settle it has always been to choose up sides and play baseball. Winner takes all. That's just how we've always done it."

Hulbert sucked in a loud gasp. "You mean to tell me if a man steals my cow, and I see him commit the act, but he won't return it because he says it's his—my only recourse is to play baseball?"

Long John Dillon led the crowd in a loud laugh. "Oh, no, sir. We would never involve baseball in petty matters such as cow rustlin'. That's what guns are for." Then John Dillon turned to the nodding crowd. "We'll let Barnaby Scrivner, our umpire-in-chief, handle the stakes. Ol' Barn runs the ball games, so he pretty much runs the town." Pointing to the crowd, he said, "Would one of you dirt screeners go upstairs and inform Barnaby of this vital matter?" Two men took off toward the stairway behind the bar.

"There'll be no need for that." The voice was sharp and somehow familiar.

The two messengers stopped at the foot of the stairs as all

heads turned toward the other end of the bar. It was Marshal Danbridge near the back wall, who had apparently been tucked away there the whole time. Rising, in all black, he cut a fearsome image. His eyes were set deep as caves under a stony-boned brow, and his face was pocked by buckshot spray, judging by the pattern of the pits.

"I am a man of the law," he said. "Impartial and honest. And seeing as I still have business in this town, I'm happy to hold the stakes."

No one objected.

Into the silence, Hulbert spoke. "I wish to see the items of gold. And the assay slips that go with them."

"I'll have all the papers and such you'll need to see delivered to you this evening, sir."

"Fine. Now, if you'll excuse us, we'd like to head next door. My men and I have had a rough ride."

"Absolutely. Take your rest."

Danbridge, too, marched along with Hulbert and the man in white, following the ballplayers out the bright red doors.

Before leaving, the marshal stopped and looked back.

"Mr. Dillon, I believe you folks harbor one more outlaw in this town I hold an interest in."

John Dillon folded his arms. "Sir, half the dirt scratchers in this room are renegades and outlaws." The men around him chuckled.

"No, no, I don't mean you bunch of two-bit church box robbers. I'm talking about a desperate outlaw. A man killer."

Dillon brought his fingers to his chin, rubbing his day-old

whiskers in deep thought. "Well, sir, all right, then." He surveyed the room with worry on his brow. "That narrows it down to 'bout fifty of us."

The men roared and chairs toppled as they rose and slapped each other's backs.

The marshal drew his gun, held it high, and fired. The room fell quiet. Wood chips drifted from the rafters.

"I'm talking, gentlemen, about a convicted murderer. Last week, he escaped from jail. A few days back, I got a glimpse of him riding this way. Goes by the name of Billy the Kid."

Jack's gut tightened. Billy lowered his head into his folded arms. The room fairly sparked as the men began to shift around and mumble.

John Dillon cracked his bat on the bar top again and bellowed, "Ain't seen 'im and wouldn't say so if I had, you no-good, tinhorn bounty snatcher. You just put a bullet through my bedroom floor! It's time for you to go." He pointed his bat at the swinging doors. "We'll get our own stakeholder."

The marshal scowled, sending an evil eye toward every man in the house. Then he left.

"I don't like him," said Jack. "He ain't a nice man."

Glancing up, Billy watched as the swinging doors stopped swinging. "Don't be too harsh on him, son. He's just another gunslinger looking to make his mark."

Not letting the marshal put a damper on things, John Dillon hefted two large travel trunks onto the bar.

"All the way from San Francisco, gentlemen. These here are our new uniforms." He opened one chest to reveal sky-blue linen shirts and white ball caps, each with a gold nugget embroidered inside the letter *D* on the front.

Whistles and cheers went up as the hats and shirts were passed around. But hoots took over when the next trunk, mostly filled with baseball knickers, also revealed a newfangled wire-basket catcher's mask and a plump catcher's mitt.

Holding the mask to his face, Blackjack Buck said, "It is to protect my good looks, *amigos*." Then he lofted the tanned-leather mitt, a "Spalding Special," thick as a tenderloin steak. "And my delicate hand."

Jack quickly doffed his felt derby and donned his short-billed baseball cap. Turning on tiptoes to see his reflection in the long mirror across the room, he said, "I'll never take this off, Billy. Even when I go to sleep!" Not knowing what to do with his old hat, Jack decided to hang it—through a bullet hole—on the horn tip of a bull's skull fastened to the wall.

Billy simply watched the hoopla around him, keeping his uniform folded in his hands.

As the commotion settled, Uncle John held up two more uniform sets. "Where's Buckles? Where's LaFay? The new men."

"Buckles walked off after the tryouts," said Jésus, "with a pocketful of rocks. Said he was going out hunting for his good-luck baseball dinner. Rabbit stew."

Uncle John shook his head. "Doggone, he's a strange one. Where's LaFay?"

"*Aquí*, Cap'n." Rico Del Rey, the team's right fielder, pointed to the last table past the bar, the one where Danbridge had been sitting. There, Mr. LaFay slumped sleepily, an empty bottle in his hand. "He's been here a little while."

"Well, all right, then," said Cap'n Dillon. "Leave 'im be. But the rest of you boys—time for church!"

The men rose in a jubilant, albeit dignified, manner. They gathered their belongings and started to file out the swinging doors.

"Church?" said Jack. "Now?"

"It's a ritual," said Fence Post. "We always go before a game. And after a game."

"And anytime in between," said Dixie Bodine.

"Well," said Billy, brushing dust from his leather vest. "It has been a while."

Jack and Billy followed the men out of the saloon and away from town. Surprisingly, though, they marched right past St. Anthony's church. Their path took them toward the Lucky Strike Mine.

"You fellows have a church in the hills?" asked Jack.

"You shall see," said Blackjack Buck. He added, "I know, for I am a prophet."

That brought a slew of laughs from the club.

"Now, son," said Dixie Bodine. "You claim to be John Dillon's nephew? Right off, I'd have to say you don't look the part."

More laughs.

"Hold on," said Blackjack Buck. "Who are you to judge?"

Dixie kept walking. "I'm just saying . . ."

"I have brothers in all colors," said the prophet. "If the cap'n takes this boy as his brother's son, who are you to question his heart?"

Dixie grinned. "I stopped doing that a long time back." He caught Jack's eye. "Welcome to your uncle's town, son."

Fence Post and a few others joined in the greeting.

Before long, the whole bunch pulled up in front of a rusty iron door chained tight against the mouth of the Lucky Strike Mine.

"You built a church in there?" asked Jack.

"Church?" said Rico. "I say it is more of a holy cathedral."

Inside the mine, it was nothing like Jack had expected. Not the dusty, crooked pathway of a heavily timbered shaft. After a short tramp down a dark passage, the "room" he stepped into was enormous. The ceiling was a curved dome, running twice as long as it was wide. Lanterns hung on the tall stone walls that went up twenty feet or more.

It was cool as a basement in there. But he saw no altar. He saw no church pews or stained glass. In fact, the only glass he saw was a dozen or so quart-sized beer mugs, rimmed in gold, all lined up on a slick wooden bar off to his right. In front of the bar sat two long benches, side by side, where the men could sit, Jack supposed, as if they were in a dugout. Along the base of the mahogany-wood bar ran a gleaming brass foot rail.

And standing behind the bar was none other than Eliza de Luz, who now wore a white cotton apron over her blue jeans, with a long white towel tucked into her belt.

"Set 'em up, barmaid," cried Long John Dillon, and the whole team rushed to the benches.

Jack stood stunned. "You boys come in here and drink beer every day? Even on the day of a game?"

"Oh, no, son," said Dixie. "We drink *root* beer. We keep it nice and cold in old oak casks deep in the mine."

"Made from cactus-apple roots," added Fence Post, "so it's plenty sweet, but, boy, it's prickly. I must warn ye. This brew has a little sting."

"Finest root beer in the land," said Lefty Wright.

Fence Post squinted, tapping a fingertip right between his eyes. "And all them ground-up cactus needles sharpen your eyesight." He winked.

"It's full of minerals, too." Tonio Wingo, the third baseman, shot his fist into the air. "Like gold!"

All the men whooped. Eliza plopped a mug down in front of Jack.

"*Gracias.*" He took a sniff. The frothy brew smelled like sweet sarsaparilla-bark juice. He took a sip. Oh, doctor! Sweet it was, but it felt like a river of thumbtacks going down.

"Whoa!" he said, then wiped the froth from his mouth with the back of his hand. Blinking back tears, he added, "That's frisky!"

The men cheered, hoisting their mugs with wolf-dog howls, then downing the sparkling liquid in one ceiling-gazing gulp.

Billy, like Jack, had been cautious. But his grin showed his pleasure, too.

Hung above the bar, glowing in the lamplight, were the solid gold bat and ball Jack had read about, mounted in a polished wood case.

"Hulbert wants to see them tonight," said Cap'n Dillon, seeming to note Jack's gaze. "Don't believe the man trusts me."

Bookending the wooden case were two open gun belts. They each held a pearl-handled pistol and were filled with scores of glittering silver cartridges.

"I hung those up long ago," the cap'n told Jack. "Got no use for 'em."

Jack could not sit. He spun off the bench and walked out into the room's center. Huge geode boulders, split in half, stood propped against the other stone wall. Inside each man-sized rock shell were hundreds of gleaming quartz crystals, row upon row, sending reflected rays of lamplight flickering out across the ceiling and walls, revealing two more side rooms.

In one chamber, at the far end, large wardrobes lined the walls.

"The last few are empty," said John Dillon, joining Jack. "Use 'em if you wish."

"I will! I'll leave my uniform in there. Boys," he called to the fellows at the bar. "This place is like a pirates' cave!"

The men roared again at that. The whole while, Billy had been resting his elbows on the bar and sipping, taking everything in. But he joined the men in that laugh.

Obviously to Jack, the Lucky Strike Mine was no longer being mined. The only dirt wall in the whole place was a small stretch between the dressing chamber and the cozy room next door to it. In that one, a dozen red velvet thrones, as stately and fine as any king had ever owned, sat snugged around a circular oak table set with silver mugs at every seat. Overhead was a golden candlelit chandelier.

"What's that room for?"

"Serious business only," said Fence Post. "For instance, after we win a game, we need to hash and rehash. So Eliza brings in a bucket of fresh ice cream and plunks a scoop into each of them steins, tops 'em off with root beer, and we set, sip, story swap, and savor."

"That's right," Eliza concurred. "And the ice cream, it floats!"

"Like a cloud in heaven," said Dixie. "A king's drink, it is."

"You have ice? And ice cream?"

"The saloon has a cellar full of ice, loaded from the lake over winter."

"Set 'em up once more, darlin'!" John Dillon walked back to the bar and slapped a twenty-dollar gold piece down on the counter—and Eliza scooped it into her apron with a laugh.

My gosh, thought Jack, rejoining the team bench. She's not only rich, but she has two of the greatest jobs in the world.

Jack caught a quick glance from Eliza. He smiled, and their look lasted long enough for her to blush. That's when someone grabbed Jack's arm.

Jésus. "To look at my sister with such eyes," he said in a tight whisper, "first you must earn my respect. So far, you have earned only a laugh."

"That's not enough, I suppose."

"That is less than not enough."

Jack nodded and quickly began calculating ways he might win that respect before he remembered he had no time for such distractions as romance.

He turned his gaze back across the room. Set between two vast geode stones he spied an open-top fifty-five-gallon brewer's keg filled with baseball bats, all shiny and looking freshly made. Next to that sat another keg decorated with glittering red and green gemstones and long bird feathers. This one was filled to overflowing with pure white baseballs—enough for a lifetime of games, Jack imagined. It was all so hard to believe.

Farther along the wall stood ten more kegs, stacked pyramid-style.

"What's in them?" asked Jack.

Fence Post gave a glance. "More root beer!" he said. "That there's our supply room."

Jack's eyes circled the glittery dome-top ceiling, the walls of crystal and stone, the bats and balls.

"This is *better* than a pirate's cave," he said. His voice softened to a whisper. "This is the holiest place on earth."

A mighty and boisterous cheer went up. Root beer flasks crashed into each other and sloshed so much sweet tonic, it nearly covered the cobblestone floor at their feet.

"Well, gentlemen," John Dillon called. He stood once again in the center of the room. "Hate to dampen the party, but we do have business to discuss."

Slowly the room came to order. The men leaned back against the bar to face their captain.

"And I suppose," he went on, "this is as good a time as any to let you fellows in on something that has weighed mightily upon my mind for several days now." He paused. His obsidian eyes studied the faces before him. "It concerns the prize we'll be playing for tomorrow when we meet those White Stockings."

"We already know about the prize," said Fence Post. "We're playing for the right to be known as the undisputed greatest team in baseball. And we'll each get a thousand dollars in cash to boot." He grinned toward all the other men sitting with their backs to the bar, who acknowledged his words with affirmations and nods.

One huge hand held aloft by their skipper brought the room to silence.

"Well, it goes a little deeper than that, boys. I suppose you realize it is not every day that a highfalutin baseball organization travels some two thousand miles to play an upstart ball club in the back hills of California."

"What are you getting at?" said Lefty. "They came. They're here."

"What I'm getting at is this. I had to sweeten the pot in order to get Mr. Hulbert to finally agree to accept our challenge."

"Sweeten the pot?" said Fence Post. "What did you do? Throw in a couple barrels of root beer?"

Everyone laughed.

"Well, yes, you might say so," Uncle John said. "We went round and round a few times, but what it all boiled down to was getting Hulbert to believe it would be worth his while for him and his boys to make this arduous trip."

Fence Post lowered his mug. "This is beginning to sound serious. What exactly did you fellows agree to?"

Long John Dillon stood silent, as if mulling the question and wishing he could flat avoid it. "What did we agree to? Plain and simple, boys. If we beat those fellows tomorrow, we not only get those bragging rights and the money, but Hulbert has agreed to place our ball team in the National League of Professional Base Ball Clubs. The highest league in the land."

"Whoa!" the men shouted, raising their glasses again. Jack could not believe what he was hearing.

Neither could Dixie, apparently. "What do you mean? All them other teams will travel way out here to play us?"

"Well, not exactly. What'll happen is, we'll take over for the Cincinnati Red Stockings. You see, Hulbert just booted them out for playing Sunday ball and selling beer at their games."

That news brought a stir to the room.

"You mean," said Jésus, "we will have to pack up and move to Cincinnati?"

"Only for about five months each year. But Jiminy Jones, half that time you'll be on the road anyhow, playing every club from the Boston Red Stockings to the Cleveland Blues."

"Hoo-whee!" yelled Lefty Wright. "Them boys, they are the major teams in the nation." More rumbles of glee.

But Dixie persisted. "You said *you* had to sweeten the pot. Sounds like Hulbert did all the sweetening."

"Well, I was getting to that." Long John Dillon spoke without a lot of enthusiasm. "If we happen to lose, I've agreed to turn this gold mine over to Mr. Hulbert."

It was as if every bit of air in that old mine and shaft had disappeared with one big gasp. The men stood wide-eyed. Jack was in shock. How could anyone risk losing a place like this?

"Cap'n," said Tonio. "You can't be serious."

"Serious as a rattlesnake in your hat."

Lefty chimed back in. "And you were just gonna spring this on us at the last minute?"

"Why'd you hold back, John?" asked Dixie.

"Well, I just found out for sure a day or so ago myself." John Dillon scanned the room. "Fact is, I didn't pay it much mind. I agreed to it because I truly believed there was no risk. We're the best team, and that was all that mattered."

"Not so fast, Cap'n," said Fence Post. "Yesterday, we were the best team. Today we've got no shortstop and we're missing the best hitter on the club."

"I understand." He stared grimly at the team.

"Why'd you even consider it?" asked Dixie. "How important is a dagburn title?"

"*Verdad,*" said Tonio. "This place, it is too much to risk."

Jésus disputed that. "Listen to you two. Did we lose already? I am with Long John. I want to play in the East, against the very best. Tomorrow, I will play shortstop. I will hit like Shadowfox. We will win!"

Jésus finished by thrusting a fist into the air, looking as if he was expecting to lead the grand cheer that would follow.

He most likely did not expect the canyon of silence and downcast eyes.

John Dillon cleared his throat. "Gentlemen, I have only this to say by way of explanation. I did not make this wager for the title. I did it because eight of you men have worked for me on the ball grounds and in my mine for a long time. And in terms of gold, you have made me rich."

Fence Post was still trying to follow. "You made us rich, too, Cap'n. We each got a cut of what this mine produced. But now you've gone and—"

"Hold it," said Uncle John. "I haven't gone and done anything except give you boys the only opportunity you will ever have to play baseball in the East at the highest level. As I was saying, you made me rich. And I saw this bargain as one way I could pay you back, not just with gold, but with the chance to live your dreams. I did it for you."

It took a moment for someone to respond, as everyone now seemed to see the picture more clearly.

"But, Cap'n," said Dixie. "You risked it all. And to a coal mine boss! Any doubt what he'll do to this countryside if he's turned loose on it?"

Uncle John's shoulders slumped, the first time Jack had ever seen the fire in the huge man burn low. "At the time," he said, "I simply had no doubt that we would win. And look at the payoff!

Snakes alive! But even our prophet, Buck, did not see this coming."

"Buck!" said Fence Post, looking about. "What happens? Do we win or lose?"

There was no answer. No words, at least. For Blackjack Buck was no longer at the bar. He had not, however, gone far.

An eerie sound, like the long one-note hoot of an owl traveling down a snowy canyon, filled the cave. It caused the men to freeze and to look toward the royal table, where Blackjack Buck stood before the red thrones, playing a long wooden flute. Only once, in the lone hills above Chaco Canyon, had Jack ever heard that haunting sound of the ancient West. That was the day the red-tailed hawks began to follow him and bring him luck. Or so he believed.

The men shifted off toward the small, dark chamber.

"What's going on?" asked Jack.

Uncle John put his hand on Jack's shoulder. "Something big. And I pray it's good. It is very unusual to be called to the throne room on a normal day."

Slowly the ballplayers—including Billy—took their seats at the exquisite round table. Carved along its edges were leafy patterns, sprinkled with hawks, rabbits, owls, bears, and coyotes.

"What is it?" said Jésus. "Why do you call us here? Do you see the game?"

Blackjack Buck set down the wooden flute and folded his hands. After looking into the eyes of everyone gathered at the table, he said, "There is one amongst us who is not what he appears to be."

Jack froze, not bothering to even glance at Billy. He didn't have to. Everyone else did.

"He is from far away," the prophet continued. "He is young. He is old. He is my brother."

"Your brother?" said Tonio. "Who? Why have you never told us?"

"Forget all that," said Fence Post. "We want to know about the game."

"Each truth has its day," said the prophet. "Now is the time to reveal these. They are the secrets of the boy of secrets." His eyes found Jack's. "You, my brother. Tell us what we need to know. Tell us the secrets of *béisbol*."

"*Me?*" said Jack.

"Him?" said Dixie. "This boy? Shoot, I got more baseball smarts in my little finger than he does in his whole self—and I ain't even *got* a little finger." He held his pitching hand aloft. The men flared out a roar.

All but Blackjack Buck. His bear-cave eyes continued to bore into Jack's.

"Me?" Jack repeated, trying to size up the situation as fast as he could. What did he mean, "his" brother? And what were "the secrets of *béisbol*"?

He felt all eyes on him. He took a deep breath. "All right then." He paused a moment. "Let me think. Secrets of baseball," he repeated, tracing a hand-carved owl on the table's edge. It had to be his secret plays, he decided. "Well, I've got so many, I'm not sure which one to start off with."

He noticed a presence at his elbow. He turned and felt relieved to see Eliza standing by his side.

"I have something for you," she said, touching his arm. "I finished it this morning." From behind her back, she produced Jack's bat. With a twist.

The men leaned in for a closer look.

Eliza set the finely polished length of blond Missouri ash on the table in front of Jack, with two horseshoes snugged evenly around the barrel, just as he had asked her to do.

"Careful," she said. "The welds are still warm." It was even better than Jack had dreamed, flame-treated from the coke fire, tinged golden brown in color, a work of art.

"What the heck kind of bat is that?" asked Fence Post.

"It's a new idea of mine," said Jack. "With the horseshoes, the bat's so barrel-heavy that if you swing it ten or twenty times just before you walk up to hit, your own bat will feel like a toothpick." He extended the iron-weighted instrument. "Here, try it."

Jésus de Luz stood alongside Eliza and beamed at his sister's handiwork. Whether he was impressed with Jack's idea, he couldn't tell, but Jésus grabbed it first.

He made his way to the bucket of bats as the players followed. At the bat barrel, they backed up and gave him room. Jésus swung the horseshoed bat a dozen times or so, then handed off Jack's invention and withdrew a wooden bat.

He got set. He swung. His eyes grew large. "This bat is like a feather. I swing ten times faster. This is magic."

Jack jumped straight up. "I told you boys. I told you! And I got a bunch more ideas where that came from."

"Come back to the throne room and tell us," said Blackjack Buck, leading the way.

While Jack returned with the men, he scanned his brain for another strategic scheme. Sitting down again, he said, "Okay, take for instance, RIM. That's R, I, M. Know what that is?"

Blank stares all around.

"'Course not. Not yet—'cause I invented it. Now listen. Suppose you're up to bat with a man on first. No outs. Well, what if the first-base coach tells the runner to make like King Kelly and steal second base?"

"But this is not new," said Tonio. "We have done this many times."

"Yes, but what does the batter do?"

Fence Post knew. "He better lay off the pitch, doggone it. Just stand there and take it, so's the runner can steal."

"Most times, that's right," said Jack. "He takes the pitch. But"—he slowly raised one finger aloft—"what if you tell the hitter to hit the ball? No matter what, just hit it some place and see what happens?"

"I like it," said Long John Dillon, finally weighing in. "Creates a little confusion for the defense. Shortstop runs to cover the stealer at second, but the ball—it might just go rolling through the hole he left behind."

"Hew-ta!" said Jack, punching his fist into the air. "Right you are. And the runner, he might end up all the way to third base, not stopping on second at all. I call it RIM. The Runner in Motion play. But that's not all."

Jack hunkered low, placing both forearms on the tabletop. He looked over each shoulder. The men inched even closer, bending over the table. "There is also a play called BRIM."

Blackjack Buck whispered his response. "What is it, my brother?"

Jack whispered back. "*Both* runners in motion. A man on first, a man on second. And they both steal."

The men straightened back up as one, sending wide eyes around the table.

"Confoundin' the opposition," said Fence Post.

"Precisely!" Jack grinned at the men, who buzzed amongst themselves.

Uncle John nodded slowly, showing deep contemplation.

Dixie Bodine, however, was not impressed. "Wait a consarn minute. It's just two men stealin' at the same time, right?"

Jack nodded. "A double steal. What's the catcher going to do?"

"Well," said Dixie, giving everyone a knowing glance, "unless he's a half-soaked goat, he'll fire the ball to third and get the lead runner."

"What if the batter hits it first?"

Dixie pulled back, rubbing his chin. "Well, chicken lizards. That changes everything."

"I tell you," said Jack, "it's high-ballin' baseball. On the train track of the future. Start the runners, boys, then say, 'Hew-ta'!"

"*Utah?*" said Lefty.

Dixie leaned forward. "Say what?"

"*Hew-ta*, boys! It's my battle cry."

Eliza repeated the shout. "Hew-ta!" She met everyone's quick glance with an openmouthed grin. "I like the way it sounds."

"What's it mean?" said Rico.

"Well, now." Jack lowered his voice to a whisper. "HEW-TA is one of the most convolutionary secrets of baseball in the world."

No one spoke a word, but their eyes shouted for more.

Jack obliged. "A man masters this one secret, even for a dozen games here or there, and he'll stand amongst the greatest players who will ever play this game."

Dixie brought down a fist. "What's it mean, dagnabbit?"

"It means, 'Hit 'em where they ain't.'"

The words seemed to take a little while to register. But then they did.

"It's poetry," said Tonio Wingo, his eyes cast high.

"It's philosophy," said Fence Post.

"It's foolishness," said John Dillon. "Who in the world can do that, time after time?"

Jack folded his arms and leaned back. "I think there might be someone in this room who can do just that."

Now the heads swiveled from Jack to each other to Jack again, trying to decipher which fellow he might be referring to.

"Okay, who is it?" said Fence Post. "Who's the HEW-TA man?"

Jack pushed back from the table and rose. "Does anybody here have a silver dollar?"

Cap Anson was fuming. Hulbert had never seen his manager—and star first baseman—so enraged, so incensed. But he let him speak.

"You are an imbecile, Toots," said Anson, shaking his finger in the plump man's face. "You write telegraph reports day after day, and don't once mention that Dillon is a black man? Are you blind, stupid, or just plain ignorant?"

He turned to Hulbert. "I am not walking onto that field tomorrow if their boy, Dillon, is going to play. Do you hear me?"

Seated at a small desk in the center of his hotel room, Hulbert took his time answering. After all, he wrote the paychecks. Allowing himself an appropriate pause to feign deep consideration, he then decided to set his angry first sacker straight.

"You will, Mr. Anson, not only perform in that game tomorrow, but cease this silly tantrum and let us get down to the serious business of going over the Dillontown lineup so the results of our match tomorrow do not disappoint." He turned to his catcher, Silver Flint, and pitcher, Larry Corcoran, the other two men in the room. "Now, I want all you fellows to take note of what Tootsie here has to say."

The men nodded.

But Anson was not finished. "I shall not perform," he said.

Hulbert glared. "Then you shall walk home, as far as I'm concerned. Leave the team. Good-bye." Pouring it on, he added, "Must I remind you, Anson, that you are the oldest man on the squad? At twenty-nine, you do not have all that many days of baseball ahead of you."

"You won't have too many either, Hulbert. None of us will, if you insist upon degrading and diluting the sport with colored men. It's gone on too long and it must be stopped. So I suggest you concern yourself with making sure John Dillon sits out tomorrow or live with the consequences. For I will surely sit the game out myself."

"Okay, I've heard enough." His patience exhausted, Hulbert leaned forward to bellow his next command. "I have no more time to waste, Anson. You will perform your full professional duties tomorrow, or your services on this club will no longer be needed. Am I clear?"

"If you fire me, I'll just go and play for Boston or Providence or for any club I wish, and they'll be happy to sign me up. And I'll get more money for my trouble."

Now Hulbert had him. He leaned back, a cat ready to begin toying with his cornered mouse.

"Aren't you forgetting something? Mr. Spalding's brilliant idea?"

"What's Al Spalding have to do with this?"

"Spalding was a great pitcher because he possessed a great

mind. And he will become a great sporting-goods magnate because he possesses a great *business* mind."

Cap Anson blew his top at that. "I'm talking about black men playing my game! Not ball gloves. Not Spalding. Besides, he would most certainly agree with me on this."

"Not entirely. Al developed a little thing called the 'Reserve List.' Remember that?"

"What's that have to do with anything? That list only allows you to reserve the five top men on your roster for next year. If you let me go, then I'm off the list and free to do as I please."

"Who said anything about letting you go?"

"You said—"

"I *said*, my good man, that your services would no longer be needed. I said nothing about letting you go. In fact, you will still be my exclusive property. And no major team in the country would dare sign you on."

"Well, then, I'll—I'll just . . ."

"You'll just have to sit out the season is what! At no pay. So don't be a fool. And don't try to pull any shenanigans on me, Anson. You're not that smart. Soon we'll have a Reserve Clause inserted into the contract of every player in the National League. I'll see to that. And you boys can either like it or lump it. This is not a game. Baseball is business, plain and simple."

Corcoran and Flint stiffened in their seats. Toots leaned back and glared.

Anson only grinned. "Well, tomorrow's match is for exhibition only. It don't count for nothing. I can walk off and it won't affect my contract none."

Hulbert pointed. "You're so hotheaded, you'd cut off your fingers to spite your hand, wouldn't you? Sit down here and shut up. Now, I'm ready to offer you a bargain, if you'll listen."

"Some bargain that'll be." Anson took his seat.

"Careful, Anson." Hulbert rose to tower over the red-haired rooster. "Look, I'm a reasonable man. Here's my offer. If you agree to honor your contract and perform in tomorrow's game, I'll make you a solemn promise. In the very near future, I'll see to it that conditions change. That there will be absolutely no black men playing National League baseball anymore, anywhere, period. We will ban them completely. Secretly, of course. But a ban, nevertheless. Now take it or leave it. I'm a busy man."

Anson looked at Toots, who closed his eyes and nodded. He looked at Hulbert. "Is this on the up-and-up?"

"I give you my word. It's been in the wind for a while. Spalding and I have discussed the matter extensively. There are a lot of top-notch black players, but in the long run, keeping them out of the game will be best for business. As baseball continues to grow, I doubt there'll be very many white people who will want to pay good money to see black men on the field. So financially, it's the wise decision."

Cap Anson shot his fierce blue eyes at Hulbert with a scowl that would have melted metal. "Then why don't you start the ban tomorrow?" He stomped to the door, yanked it open, and slammed it shut behind him.

The glass in the hotel room chandelier tinkled, sending candlelight dancing on the walls.

"Well," said Toots, "he may regret this rather quickly. He can't exactly catch a train out of here tomorrow. I wager he'll be back."

"Not my problem." Hulbert, as promised, wasted no more time. "Flint, you're my captain tomorrow. Can we work around the loss of Anson?"

Silver Flint, a tall, stately man of few words, nodded once. A veteran catcher who had vowed on principle never to wear a catching glove, he folded his gnarled hands and leaned closer. "We can bring Goldsmith in to play first base, since he won't be pitching. Not the hitter Anson is, but he should do fine against these galoots."

"Good," said Hulbert. "Done. Now then, Toots, let's go down the Dillontown lineup, player by player. Tell us what you know about each, and Corcoran, write this down and study on it. I want no mistakes from the pitcher's box tomorrow. We should beat these boys walking away."

Toots started off his portion of the session by declaring, "Yes, well, as you men may have heard, a well-placed rattlesnake has taken their star shortstop out of the match, and a timely telegraph sent by yours truly to an Arizona lawman has taken their star batsman out of left field."

Since the poor man seemed to be begging for it, Hulbert pointed a job-well-done finger at Toots.

Pleased, he continued. "I spent all morning spying on the

Dillontown Nine to see what steps they'd be taking to shore up their team. They added a few players, but I've already paid off two of them to sandbag the game. And another one's just a boy. But the one last fellow has me worried. However, I'm working on a plan. Beyond that, I don't foresee too much of a problem handling the rest of them. So here goes."

The four men strategized for more than an hour until Hulbert sat convinced that Larry Corcoran, his starting pitcher, knew the strengths and weaknesses of each hitter, top to bottom.

"De Luz, he's a sucker for the inside pitch."

"Wingo couldn't hit a curveball if it was a slow boat coming 'round a river bend."

"With Buck and Dillon, keep everything low and away."

He made certain his catcher, Silver Flint, also knew the overall strategy to apply to the game.

"Knock 'em down, kick 'em around, and don't let 'em know what hit 'em," said Hulbert. "That's my philosophy, in business and in life, and it has never failed me yet."

Long John Dillon handed Jack three silver dollars. Grinning, Jack accepted the coins, placing two in his pocket. He caught Billy's eye. Billy, who had kept a low profile to this point, stared a moment, then grinned slightly. To Jack's delight and relief, he gave a secret nod.

Jack walked from the throne room to the stretch of dirt wall just outside and stopped. The softer surface, he decided, would provide the best background for what he had in mind.

"Men," Jack began as he turned to the gang who had followed him. "You all know it takes great skill to hit a baseball. Patience, timing, coordination of hand and eye." He held the silver piece in the air for all to see. "But what does it take to hit one of these? With a bullet?"

Before anyone could answer, Jack tossed the coin into the air, high overhead, so high it climbed almost to the ceiling dome.

Everyone watched as it arced up, then began to fall. No one saw Billy, at the back of the crowd, draw his gun and fire.

Blam!

The shock waves filled the cavern. The players hunched over, and some dropped to the cobblestones. The coin suddenly flew sideways, crashed into the wall, then fell to the stone floor as well.

Everyone seemed to follow the tinkle of sound, metal upon stone, until the coin stopped and died.

Jack walked a few steps, picked it up, and held it to his eye—peering at the men from a bullet hole right through the bun on Miss Liberty's head.

"Well, I'll be doggone," said Fence Post. He hacked out a laugh.

"Let me see this," said Jésus, reaching out to Jack. The whole team moved foward to get a better look.

"Men," said Jack, handing the coin to Jésus, *"that's* what it takes to hit a silver dollar—or a baseball—anywhere you want, especially *where they ain't.* Perfect eyes, perfect timing. And I think this man can do it more times than not."

Now the focus of attention was on Billy. And the suspicion.

"Where'd you learn to shoot like that?" asked Dixie. "I've heard of that trick, but never known a fellow who felt it necessary to learn how."

John Dillon moved forward, addressing Billy. "Not too many men can handle a gun like that. Takes a lot of practice." He narrowed his eyes. "Type of thing a gunslinger might work on."

"My friend Bill Henry," said Jack, going into protective mode, "once rode with Buffalo Bill's Wild West Show, boys. He knows all sorts of tricks."

Billy did not exactly back him up, nor did he contradict. He simply shook his head, reholstered his pistol, and walked back to the table of thrones.

"Show's over, gentlemen," he said. "I'm a one-trick pony."

"What was that name again?" said Fence Post.

Billy answered ahead of Jack. "Bill Henry."

"I once knew a John Henry," said Dixie, "down South. He was a steel-drivin' man."

"Oh, yeah," said Jack, butting in. "I heard of him, too."

"No relation," said Billy. He turned to Jack. "What was your point, son?"

"Well, my point is, for a fellow to hit a ball precisely where he wants it to go, he must display a quickness that is beyond the range of most men. But I believe, with scientific practice, certain men can learn to do it."

"An outlaw," said Jésus, "might have quickness like that." He was not smiling.

"If you're saying something here," said Fence Post, "say it, Jésus. Do you suspect this fella of being Billy the Kid?"

Spoken aloud, the suggestion, which Jack knew they'd all been thinking, sent a chill through the room.

"Ha!" he said. "That's a good one. Everybody knows Billy the Kid stands six foot six and weighs about two forty-five."

This time Billy helped. With a smile, he said, "I heard the same thing."

"Fellows," said John Dillon. "It wouldn't make one whit of difference if this boy's name was Jesse James. We got a ball game to win." He turned to Billy. "Son, I'll keep your quickery in mind. But I will also say, once this game is played, you're on your own. If there's a price on your head, I cannot guarantee what any man in this town—or this room—might do. Do we understand each other?"

Billy sprouted a slight grin. Tucking his thumbs into his gun belt, he closed his eyes and nodded.

"So for the rest of you," the cap'n went on, "we got the game of our lives tomorrow, and we need to look ahead. To the likes of King Kelly, Cap Anson, and this little five-foot-two double-barreled pitcher named Corcoran."

As the team's skipper took over the meeting, Jack was happy to step back and let the big man work. Everything, it seemed, was falling into place.

After the clubhouse meeting wrapped up, Long John Dillon invited Jack and Billy back to his place for dinner.

"Really?" asked Jack. "Both of us?"

"What kind of question is that?" the man growled. "I said so, didn't I?"

"Yes, sir."

Long John grabbed both ballplayers by the backs of their necks, guiding them along. "If we're sharing a dugout, I figured we might as well get acquainted."

However, Jack saw no hint of playfulness in the man's face. This, he felt, would be more than a social affair.

"We'll send down for a couple T-bone steaks," the cap'n added. "How's that sound?"

Both Jack and Billy agreed that it sounded fine.

On the way to the Touch 'Em All, John Dillon cocked back his head and spoke to the sky above.

"Baseball moon tomorrow, boys. I ought not say so, but I am a bit superstitious. I scheduled this game for Sunday, not just to get Hulbert's goat, but because I knew that moon would be rising over the center-field crowd just about game time."

"It's good luck for the home team," Jack said to Billy. "Unless the clouds roll in and the moon disappears. Then it's bad luck."

Billy read the sky in a glance. "Clear as a bell up there. I think we'll have us a lucky day."

As they reached Maine Street, Jack felt a puff of wind riffle his cheeks. Just a puff. And it was a warm wind, from the east. Dry. Not a wind bringing clouds. His father had taught him early in life that it was always good for a ballplayer to know which way the wind was blowing. And tonight it was blowing his way.

Approaching the doors of the saloon, Jack noticed that, even on the boardwalk outside, his knees were shaking from the lively piano music and foot stomping traveling through the floorboards from inside. Things had certainly grown more raucous since the afternoon.

Upon entering, Billy told Jack and the cap'n that he wanted to try his luck at a card game before joining them upstairs.

"Suit yourself," John Dillon shouted above the roar. "Be careful. Plenty of cardsharps in this town."

"Yeah," said Jack. "And don't take no wooden nickels."

"Yes, sir," said Billy, waving to both as he quickly disappeared toward his usual spot at the front corner of the crowded saloon.

Making their way to the staircase behind the bar, John Dillon asked Jack, "Where are you two boys staying?"

"We have a camp on the edge of town. Billy—uh, Bill Henry—he likes it that way."

"Oh, he does," said the man, his tone seeming to say more than he had said. "Well, let me know if you should ever desire more civilized accommodations."

"Yes, sir, I will."

Once inside Long John Dillon's suite, Jack felt instantly at home. Somehow, the comfort of the furnishings and the warmth of the rooms gave him a feeling of being accepted. Of being welcomed. Understood.

He fell into his "usual" chair.

"I understand about the ball game now, sir. Why you did what you did. Not just so your boys can become the Cincinnati Red Stockings, but to save the mountains from being washed away."

Uncle John set a bottle on the small table next to him. He poured himself a short drink. "Son, I risked so much because there comes a time in a man's life when he realizes that sittin' back and doing nothing but hoping for the best is riskier than gambling all you got. Of course, that was before I lost two top men. Now one of them lies in the infirmary part petrified, and the other is in the next bed over, in a coma. And I don't honestly know which'll come first, a ball game or a funeral. I did not count on that."

The man sipped his drink, leaned back, and folded his arms across his chest. "I just cannot bear the thought of that coal miner Hulbert going in there and blasting out every last bit of gold. I have seen it, son. They blow open the hillside and wash it down with high-pressure water, day and night. Then they haul the rock ore to the stamping mills, and they run them noisy clang-and-bang barns twenty-four hours a day as well, grinding everything to dust until the whole mountain runs down the river valley. Soon nothing is left but destruction."

"And a million dollars," said Jack.

"Pardon?"

"Eliza thought there might be a million dollars of gold still in there."

"Yes," said the cap'n, leaning forward, "that may be true. But it will take five hundred workers many a year to get it out, all laboring for penny wages. Don't fool yourself, son. No one makes any money on all that crippling, backbreaking labor except the owner of the mine. And I won't have an operation like that in these hills. I won't have any man working for slave wages if I can help it."

"But if you win this game," said Jack, "the town loses its team."

"They lose *this* team. But I can always build them another one."

"But you won't be here. You and me, we'll be playing in the major baseball league of the nation."

Jack was a little surprised when Uncle John did not take his bait and begin spouting plans and dreams of what the Dillon boys could do to the baseball world given the big chance.

Instead, he put his fingers to his chin and stared right into Jack's eyes.

"Let's not get ahead of ourselves, son. There'll be time for everything."

"Yes, sir."

"As I said, I did this for my men. To give them an opportunity I never had." He drained his glass.

Jack had nothing more to say. He couldn't wait to get Billy up here, to at least add a little distraction to the situation.

They heard a knock at the door.

John Dillon turned. "Well, that must be supper. I hope you're hungry, son. These are mighty big steaks."

It was a relief for Jack to switch focus. And whether this man was his father's brother or not, in spirit or in truth, Jack now knew that the man was in great need of a family—and Jack was honored to be so considered.

Behind that door was not only a kitchen chef with a dinner tray, but a dessert delivery as well. Eliza joined them, carrying a shiny metal bucket sweating with drops of water. Tonight, she wore a long cotton dress and fancy girl-shoes instead of boots! The buttoned-down flaps had scalloped edges, and there were little leather shoofly tassels on the toes.

Seeing her looking so elegant had him sorely tongue-tied.

Removing the bucket lid, she showed Jack a mound of white ice cream, a delight he had tasted only once in his life.

"You just whipped it up?" he blurted, marveling at the lush cream. "Just like that?"

She tilted her head and widened her eyes at the ridiculous question.

Oh, too, too bad, Jack thought, looking at her and what she held. That is, too bad he had no time for romance. Because it would not take much coaxing to get a boy like him to fall for a girl who knew the secret of making ice cream.

They all stood where the meal was placed, in the formal dining room, around a large table.

"I guess I should go down and get Billy," said Jack. "He won't want to miss this."

"No, you stay here," said Eliza, who most certainly had seen the way Jack had stared at the dessert. "I will go get him."

Before Jack could offer at least a polite protest, she was gone.

And he missed her already.

This better be good, Toots." Hulbert placed both elbows on the barroom table set in the back of the hall. He flicked his lighter twice and lit his cigar.

"I was all settled in and doing quite well in my room, and now you drag me down here, among the riffraff swilling their sagebrush whiskey like lunatics." Hulbert turned to Marshal Danbridge, sitting next to him. "No offense, Marshal."

Danbridge grunted and downed his amber shot of popskull.

"You recall," said Vernon Toots, leaning across the table, "that I expressed concern today regarding one new ballplayer on the Dillontown Nine."

"You said you had a plan."

"I said I was working on one. But again it may be somewhat extreme." He looked at Hulbert as if expecting a reaction. Or permission.

Hulbert puffed, then barked, "Why so?"

"Because this wily fellow displayed the skill and nerves of steel I have seen only in champions. He has a shrewdness and a coolness and a quickness no one—not King Kelly, not Cap Anson—no one can match."

Hulbert huffed, then puffed again. "Well, there's an easy fix to that." His eyes roamed the noisy room from behind a fresh cloud of smoke. "Make the man a Chicago White Stocking. That would solve our Cap Anson problem right there, wouldn't it? Go make your 'Mr. Nerves of Steel' an offer."

"I already tried that. He turned me down cold. And these local boys got rather nasty about it."

"So we don't want to see this new fellow on that ball field tomorrow," said Hulbert, growing impatient. "Is that what all this is leading up to?"

"I feel it would be wise. Mr. Danbridge took care of Shadowfox Coe for us, and if you concur, I propose he do the same with this one."

Hulbert turned to the marshal. "I don't want to know the details, Danbridge. Just tell me this. Can you guarantee this fellow will be no problem for us?"

"That I can."

"Fine. Do what you have to do." It seemed to Hulbert a simple matter. "We'll pay you the same money we paid for the removal of Mr. Coe."

Danbridge nodded.

"Marshal," said Toots, rising slowly from his chair. "I will show you our boy. Do you see that far game in the corner by the window? Full of ballplayers wearing their brand-new caps? He's the young blond fellow who's talking to the Mexican girl."

Danbridge rose up alongside Toots and searched the far corner with cold eyes.

"We want no fuss," said Toots. "After he leaves the game,

make sure you get off alone with him and then"—he paused for effect—"turn out the lights. Understand?"

Danbridge said nothing. Slowly a wicked grin filled his face. "Mr. Toots, this is going to be easier than you think." He drew his gun.

Toots grabbed Danbridge's arm. "Are you insane? Put that thing away."

Danbridge sloughed him off and walked crisply toward the poker game.

Now Hulbert stood, sending two bull snorts of smoke out of his nose, one streaming left, one right. "What's got into him?"

Before Toots could respond, the entire barroom fell silent at the sight of Danbridge standing ten paces from the ballplayer, his arm extended, his weapon drawn.

"Freeze, Kid! Don't move a muscle. You there, *señorita*, step aside."

The girl straightened, but did not step back. Instead, she froze, wide-eyed with fear.

The young ballplayer looked up over his hand of cards, sighted Danbridge, then looked down again, as if he were still trying to decide whether he should hold, fold, or draw.

"You still here, Danbridge?" the young man muttered. "Thought you'd be long gone by now. Weren't you told to *adios*?"

"Would the snake charmer leave without his snake? Why don't you tell these folks how much of a snake you are? How you killed man after man. Arizona, New Mexico. And how much money you've got on your head."

There was a rustle in the room as the rugged clientele shifted positions to get a better look.

"Who is he?" someone said.

"Just a young fella," said another.

Danbridge's eyes never left the gambler. "Thought you could hide out in a town full of fools and buffoons, didn't you?"

One old gambler took umbrage at that remark. "Who you calling a fool, Danbridge?"

"Shut up!" Again he glared at the young man. "Why don't you tell these folks your name? Pick one. You've had quite a few, as I recall."

"It's him," another man said in a harsh whisper. "It's got to be. That's Billy the Kid."

Hulbert had never seen a jolt of electricity rifle-blast through a room as it did upon the utterance of the outlaw's name. The girl fairly swooned, her knees buckling into the outlaw's leg as she placed both palms on the table to steady herself.

"Billy Bonney," Danbridge called, with glee in his voice, "alias, Billy the Kid, I place you under arrest for escape from prison. And I'm taking you, a duly convicted murderer, back to Santa Fe, New Mexico, where you're gonna hang."

Billy the Kid dropped his cards. "Gentlemen," he said, addressing the other players at his table, "it appears I will have to fold." He slowly raised his hands.

Hulbert watched, intrigued, as Billy the Kid sat calmly, looking straight into the barrel of the gun. He'd never seen the like. This was one cool customer.

Danbridge moved closer to the table, and as he approached, all the card players seated there pushed back and scrambled away. The girl did not move. Her arms trembled. She now seemed as if she were about to faint.

"Somebody get that girl out of here," said Danbridge, waving his gun. "Kid, you stand, slow and easy."

An older man stepped forward. "Eliza," he said, reaching out to take the frightened girl by the arm as Billy the Kid rose. At the touch of the man's hand, however, the girl screamed, pulling away and falling back into the Kid.

Instantly, he grabbed her around the waist as a shield, drew his firearm, and began dragging her toward the door.

"That girl won't save you, Kid." Danbridge swung his pistol at the pair as they moved in front of him.

In a flash, two cardplayers rose with guns drawn. Toward Danbridge.

"Drop it, Danbridge!" yelled one gruff mountain man built like a beer keg with a ball cap on his head. "You shoot anywhere near that girl, and your bones'll be bleaching on Dog's Ridge by noontime tomorrow."

The marshal froze, then slowly lowered his arm.

Billy the Kid kept moving. "No one follows me," he shouted, "or the girl dies." He continued dragging the petrified girl backward through the swinging doors and onto the boardwalk. Firing twice into the air, he shouted again. "No one follows me, you hear? Or you die, and the girl does, too."

As one more shot and the sound of running boots on the

boardwalk filled the night, Hulbert turned to Toots, who was still shaking at the series of events.

"Relax, old boy," said Hulbert. He grinned as he tapped the ashes from his cigar onto the floor. "That solves our 'Mr. Nerves of Steel' problem quite nicely, doesn't it? And it won't cost me a cent."

28

"I thought I'd gotten rid of Danbridge yesterday," said John Dillon, standing at the foot of the stairs, surveying the nearly empty barroom in front of him. The silence in the saloon earlier that evening had caught the attention of Jack and the saloon owner. The gunshots had brought them downstairs.

"Well," said Jack, "I guess he wasn't going to leave without Billy."

Long John Dillon placed his hand on Jack's shoulder. "So you're finally ready to admit the truth. Your friend, Bill Henry—is Billy the Kid."

"Yes, sir. I'm sorry I lied about that. He asked me to keep things hush-hush."

"Well, I don't fault you on that. Right now I fault myself. I looked past his reputation, hoping to empower my team, and now—" He drew a hard, fast breath. "I just may have cost a young girl her life."

"Billy won't hurt her, sir. Don't worry. He wouldn't do that."

"Son, the man is an outlaw who has already proved he will do anything it takes to stay alive. If that had been you instead of

Eliza, he would have done the same thing. Think about it. Ever since you trailed up with him, hasn't he been using you as a shield as well?"

"No, no. No, sir. I'm his scout. My job is to—" Suddenly, Jack felt completely foolish. Hornswoggled. He turned away. After all, wasn't a scout just another name for the guy who gets shot at first? Still, Jack could not believe Billy would cause Eliza any harm.

Half the team had been playing poker in the saloon that night and had scattered through the town chasing after the pair, but with no results. Later, four of them—Tonio, Dixie, Fence Post, and Blackjack Buck—returned to work out a better plan to track Billy and bring Eliza back home.

"We're almost certain they're still on foot, Cap'n," said Fence Post. "His horse is still in the barn, and no one saw anyone ride out of town."

"They've surely split up by now," said Long John. "Any sign of the girl?"

"Not yet. Jésus is still searching the town with Danbridge." Turning to Jack, Fence Post added, "We need to know where you boys are camped out."

"I'll take you there," said Jack, "but we ought to be careful. No telling what he might do." He could not believe he was uttering those words. But he did not doubt them either.

Jack led the four-man posse of ballplayers up into the campsite. He went in first, but there were no signs of Billy or Eliza, or any signs that they had been there.

"I have a hunch," said Blackjack Buck as they traveled the trail back to town.

"Well, one of your hunches trumps most people's facts," said Dixie. "Shoot."

"There is one place most people won't look."

"*Ay,*" said Tonio. "Good idea. We will search all the outhouses!"

"No," said Blackjack Buck, freezing the posse. "The holy cathedral. She has a key."

The posse found the gate to the Lucky Strike unlocked. The chain had been pulled tight and the padlock was in place, but upon inspection, they saw it was not set. That was enough to cause them to draw their guns.

"Wait," said Jack. "No guns. Let me go in. I'll talk to him. I'll get him to let her go."

"You'll get yourself killed, is what'll happen," said Dixie. "And her, too. I say we stay put and wait him out."

Tonio did not like that idea. "He might not even be in there."

"What do you propose?" said Fence Post.

Tonio shrugged. "Send the boy in."

Now Dixie protested. "You can't send a boy in to do a man's job."

"Hey, wait a minute," said Jack. "I'm seventeen years old."

"What?" Dixie led the entire posse in casting a sharp glance Jack's way.

"Well, nearly."

"Well, soon's you boys get done arguing, you can *all* come in." It was Billy, calling out from inside the cavern.

Not only had Billy known they were out there, but once they walked inside, Jack realized they had all been expected. Half a dozen mugs were filled with root beer. Eliza was behind the bar singing to herself, and Billy greeted them with a grin.

"We would have had some ice cream for you boys, but my ace sidekick here left it back at the hotel."

"*Sí,*" Eliza called out. "Billy is thinking that it could be now the time to get a new sidekick."

"What are you talking about?" Jack looked around in alarm. "What'd I do wrong?"

"Not so fast," said Fence Post. "Kid, you got some explaining to do."

"Right," said Jack. "The whole town is out gunning for you, Billy. As far as they know, you killed Eliza and hotfooted it into Old Mexico. I just saved your life. I threw everyone off your trail by going to the old campsite." He caught harsh looks from the posse for that little stretch. "Well, I did, didn't I?"

"Shoo-shoo, all of you. *Silencio,*" said Eliza. "As you can see, he did not kill me very good." She had an unusually haughty tone to her voice. "The truth is, *I* saved *his* life. The plan of escape, it was all my idea."

"What?" said Jack.

"Yep." Billy nodded in full agreement with Eliza. "I was actually planning to go along with Danbridge all peaceful like, hoping you boys might tag along. Since I knew this town had no justice of any doggone peace, I figured it couldn't have much of a jail."

That drew a welcome laugh.

"He is right," said Tonio. "We do not. We have a dugout behind Tia Rosa's Cantina. But it has been dug out of many times."

Everyone laughed even louder.

"I only thought," said Eliza, "this Danbridge, he will kill Billy. So I jumped to him and made him take me away." Her eyebrows lowered into a scold aimed at her brother's teammates. "Do you think I would faint at such a time? You do not know me better than this?"

No one bothered to answer.

Billy turned to Jack. "She's a quick thinker, son. I tell you, your sidekicking days may be over."

"Wait, you can't do that. Her? She's just a girl." Ah, those words! Too late. He could not get them back.

"Just a girl?" Eliza glared. "Oh, so you think you could do what I did."

Jack backed up, speechless, brainless.

"It don't matter what she is, son." Billy grinned, enjoying this. "Quick thinkers come in all varieties."

Eliza wiped her hands on her towel, flung it at the bar top, and said, "Somebody else must clean up. I need to find my brothers before they go *loco*. And if Jésus, he comes here, tell him I have gone home." She hurried toward the door.

"Darlin'?" called Billy playfully. "Say, if you can help it, please don't let anybody else see you. Let them think we're miles away."

Eliza bent her knees and stopped. Swiveling around with a mischievous grin, she did not answer or even look at Billy. Instead she addressed the huddle of men.

"I think I am in love with him."

"You *are*?" Once again, the words shot out, escaping Jack's lips before he could stop them.

"Oh, shoo-shoo," she said, waving her hand high. "I am only yoshing."

"Oh." He looked around at the men, already snorting and grinning. "Not that it would matter none to me," he added, coughing into his hand. "Why would I give an owl's hoot?"

Eliza paused at the passageway to the door. "Do not worry, Billy. These people, they know me. If they see me, I will say I fought like a wildcat and escaped. And that you are long gone. They will believe me."

Quickly she caught Jack's eye. To him she said, "Everyone believes me."

Everyone watched her go.

"Some girl," said Billy.

"And you are some outlaw," Fence Post said in such a way that Jack could not tell if it was praise or disgust.

At any rate, he defended Billy. "He ain't as bad as people say, boys."

"He ain't?" said Dixie. "Killed a dozen men, I heard."

"Oh, that's just what the newspapers say. They lie. Same as the politicians." Jack winked at Billy, who only glanced away.

"This boy is right," said Blackjack Buck.

"I am? I mean, yes, I am."

Dixie interrupted. "What do you know about Billy the Kid, Buck?"

The prophet approached Billy with a flat stare, giving nothing away. Standing face to face, Blackjack Buck said, *"Hola,* El Chivato."

"Hola, amigo."

"El Chivato?" asked Fence Post.

"In Mexico," said the prophet, "this man, he is known as the kid, the little goat, El Chivato. He is much loved in Mexico."

"Ay," said Tonio. "It is true."

"No fooling?" Fence Post scratched his head. "Why is that?"

"We admire anyone," explained Blackjack Buck as he turned around, "who stands up to a dishonest government. First he fights the crooked cattlemen who run Lincoln County in New Mexico. Then it is the governor of New Mexico himself. This man, he makes a promise to Billy. He will grant a full pardon if Billy will testify against a cold-blooded murderer. Billy did."

"Yes, sir. I did." On the bench, leaning his back against the bar, Billy decided to get involved.

"He took a great risk," Blackjack Buck continued, "but the governor, he breaks his word."

"Yes, sir. He did." Billy stressed the point with a thrust of his mug.

"El Chivato should be a free man today. Instead he is hunted like a dog under a chicken house. And my people, we always side with the underdog."

Jack stood slack-jawed, incredulous. "You never told me any of that."

Billy shrugged. "Would it have made a difference?"

"No, I guess not." Jack paused a moment. "But you should be a free man. And it's hard to believe a top official would lie like that."

"Like I say," said Billy, who had to say no more.

Jack stepped closer. "So, will you be at the game tomorrow?"

"How can he do that?" asked Tonio.

"Right, son," said Fence Post. "Danbridge is sure to be around."

"Or some other bounty snatcher." Dixie sneered the words.

"Not if they think Billy's in Mexico." Jack raised his eyebrows.

Fence Post saw the flaw in that. "How long until someone spots him at the game? Folks know him now. By sight."

"Oh, yeah," said Jack. "That could be a problem."

"Stay here tonight, Kid," said Fence Post. "There's bedding in the supply room you can drag out. May smell like me, but it's softer than these rocks."

"Much obliged."

Blackjack Buck offered a more long-term solution. "We will bring your horse to you at daybreak. You would be wise to ride into Old Mexico. And wiser still if you never came back."

"I'll be gone at first light, gentlemen. And again, I thank you."

Jack would not leave Billy alone—not if he were riding away in the morning. As soon as the other men left, Jack addressed his biggest concern.

"You can't leave here, Billy."

"Why not?"

"Well, first off, because I'm your scout and I'd have to go with you. Then we'd both miss the game."

"Son, truthfully. Your sidekicking days are over."

"But—but, that can't be. I'm just getting started. And you still have so much to teach me."

"I do? Like what, shooting my way out of town? Oh, I forgot, you know about that already. What then, escaping from jail?"

That actually had been one of Jack's ideas. "Well, maybe later. But—" He stopped to rake through the tangle in his brain. "Well, for instance, what about shooting a silver dollar in midair? Billy, I need to learn that."

"You need to learn that like a fish needs a pair of boots."

"No, you don't understand. It's the quickness of hand and eye, the timing, the coordination."

"You have all those skills."

"Not like you."

Billy looked up at the dirt wall across the room, seeming sorry now he'd ever been roped into the shooting display.

"Look," he said, "it took me six months of solid shooting to get the hand and eye for it."

"But I already have good hands and eyes. And we have all night."

"No, we don't. I'm hittin' the hay. Got a big day of riding tomorrow."

Jack hated to hear that. His mind whirled into cyclone speed. "If you're leaving, and I'll never see you again, then I wish you'd take a little time on our last night together to show me just enough of how you do it, so I can at least practice the shot on my own." He peeked up at Billy to see how he was taking his plea. Billy was unmoved, so he went on, sorrowing up his voice into a choke. "You know, to give me something to remember you by."

Billy shook his head, looking off. "Then you'll let me sleep in peace?"

"I promise."

"I'll probably need a hundred rounds just for lesson one."

"Oh." Jack knew Billy's gun belt had a dozen or two. He looked around. "That many? What if people start to hear?"

"Highly doubtful. Out here? Through those walls?"

Jack grinned. Billy was actually helping. "Okay, then. What about them gun belts above the bar?"

Billy glanced. "Might be enough."

"So you'll do it?"

"Let's get started, son."

It did not take long for Billy to lose the edge to his voice and assume the role of teacher. It was the part of him Jack liked the most.

"Anticipate," he kept telling Jack. "Anticipate the arc and the fall. Then get out ahead of it with your shot. And don't yank the trigger. Squeeze it, nice and easy. Not too soon, not too late. Anticipate."

Billy worked with Jack for more than two hours, showing him how to hold the pistol, to balance it in his hand, to time the shot just right, constantly reminding him that "You don't pull the trigger. You squeeze. One smooth motion."

And out of seventy-five shots, Jack was able to hit the dollar coin only once. It was the last shot.

"Oh, now I get it," he said. "That was easy."

Billy was already heading for the supply room to see what he might find to use for a bed that night. Jack could tell his mind was somewhere miles away. Returning, he tossed Jack a few blankets, then shook out a rug for himself.

Silently, they prepared for sleep.

Jack blew out the final lamp. The room was pitch black.

He made his way back to his bedding, then sat and tugged off his shoes. After fixing a makeshift pillow, he lay back. Then, into the ceiling dome, he said, "Billy?"

"Yeah, son?"

"Do you think a guy could steal home?"

Billy offered a quick sigh. "Could you maybe ask me that in the morning?"

"I think it almost is morning."

"That's what I'm getting at. Son, it's late."

"Well, I know. But I was just asking."

Billy took a moment to respond. "Well, what. You mean, a runner on third base trying to steal while the pitcher is tossing the ball?"

"Right."

"Yeah, well, think about it. The catcher would already have the ball, wouldn't he? So, no good. It'd be suicide."

"But not if you could beat the ball home."

"Son, you really have to think this one out for yourself."

"But Billy, I *have* been thinking about this. If you time it just right—catch the pitcher napping, not paying you any mind—I say it might work."

"He'd have to be taking a *siesta*. That ball gets there in no time."

"Still," said Jack, imagining the scenario as best he could. "If the runner times it right. Like tonight, how you taught me to pull the trigger. At one certain moment?"

"You don't pull a trigger, remember? You squeeze."

"Right, but I just mean the timing. Start moving—start squeezing—the moment the pitcher starts, so he can't get you."

"Well, I don't know."

"I think I'll call it the squeeze play."

Jack could hear Billy shuffle, as if turning from one side to the other.

"Call it what you want," Billy finally said. "But, listen. They can always get you. And don't ever forget it. If you do, they'll get you every time."

"Billy?"

"Son, I was sleeping."

"I know, but I—I just had one more question." Jack took Billy's silence as permission to proceed. "Do you miss your brother?"

Jack heard Billy shift around. Cough. "Makes you ask that?"

"Just wondering."

"Suppose. Some."

"Because I had a brother."

"You did, huh?"

"Died with my folks."

"Oh, right. Desperado. Blaze of gunfire. G'night, pardner."

"No, no." Jack waited a moment before deciding it would be okay. Okay to tell Billy the truth. Right here. This truth. On their last night together.

"It was with the water disease," said Jack. "Diptheria. Took all three of them. It is a horrid thing."

Billy responded rather unexpectedly. "It is, isn't it? I know about that. You're saying the truth, aren't you?"

"Yes, sir." Somehow Billy knew, thought Jack. He could tell.

"Back in St. Louis?"

"Yes, sir. Outside there. Town of La Croix."

"I'm sorry, son. Terrible sorry." After a goodly pause, he added, "You don't have to tell me any more truth if you don't want to. All right?"

Jack nodded, though he knew he could not be seen, for by then his throat had clutched up on him something fierce.

There was more rustle from Billy's spot, more low, slow breathing. Getting resettled, Jack figured. And he thought some more about his brother, playing toss with his brother, Fain. Running a squeeze play with Fain. How they would do it. And he heard no more from Billy.

Then, just before sleep, Billy's gentle voice broke the silence.

"I do, son," he said. "My brother. I miss him. Miss him more than I just let on."

Jack squeezed his arms against his chest, forcing his shoulders up, as if a chill had ghosted through the room.

"Me, too," he said softly, and that was all. He let the tears warm his face.

The next morning around dawn, Cap'n Dillon and Blackjack Buck threw open the huge cavern door.

"Wake up, boys." The skipper's boots cracked against the gritty sand on the stone floor. "We got breakfast. *Chorizo con huevos*, fresh from Rosie's."

Jack sat up, squinting into the graylit room, spotting the cap'n holding a basket covered with a towel.

"Whoo-hoo." Jack looked around for Billy.

He was gone. His bedding was gone, everything.

"Billy left already?" asked Jack, sitting up. "Did you see him?" Jack had not realized how hard it would hit him.

John Dillon turned to Blackjack Buck with the same question in his eyes. The prophet stared back. "I thought he was here."

Jack's heart plummeted deep into his stomach. "He didn't even say good-bye. How could he leave without saying good-bye?" He finger-combed his hand through his hair, gripping his neck.

"Well," said John Dillon, setting the basket on the bar top, "I suppose he saw his chance and he took it. But it's quite a walk from here to Old Mexico. We still have his horse. And truly, we came here to warn him."

"Warn him of what?"

"Not to go. Danbridge has lookouts stationed from Dog's Ridge to Rattlesnake Peak and every saloon and card room in between. He wants that reward money."

"Then Billy should be right here. Inside the church. It's the only place he'd be safe."

"I tend to agree." The groggy voice came from behind the bar. Billy!

Jack ran around to see. "What're you doing back there?"

"Trying to get some sleep. Son, you talk as much while you're snoozing as you do when you're awake."

"No, I don't. I mean, I was dreaming, that's all." He gave Blackjack Buck a solemn look. "I was having a vision."

Billy stuck a finger in his ear, retrieving something. "Well, I had to put sound-killers in my hearing holes, it got so bad." He held up two bullets, one in each hand.

"Doggone it, Billy." Jack kicked at the rumpled bedding. "We thought you ran off."

Billy stood up. "I just about did. But I'm glad I stayed, according to what you fellows just said about our friend Danbridge."

"He's determined to get you," said the cap'n. "And there's not a whole lot we can do about it. But you're welcome to stay in here, far as I'm concerned, until he gives up and rides off."

Billy grinned. "*Chorizo* and eggs and all the root beer I can drink? Watch out, I might not ever leave."

"Billy," said Jack. "You *should* never leave." He turned to Blackjack Buck. "I'm sorry, I'm going against your advice that he should head to Old Mexico. But last night, that thought just came to me."

"Don't worry," said Billy. "The both of you. I got plans to make a new home for myself. In good country. Got it all worked out."

As the morning wore on, the rest of the team trickled in, until by noon or so, the whole gang was there, dressed and ready to play the game.

"The band's outside, Cap'n," Dixie called from the doorway. "They're ready to escort us to the field."

"Tell 'em to go on into town ahead of us and play for the people. We don't need no parade this time. But we do want those folks fired up. We'll be coming 'round the corner right soon, tell 'em."

Dixie retreated. Uncle John called the rest of the team close.

"We need this one, boys," the cap'n began. "We need it bad. And I'll tell you one more reason why. Six years ago this very day—on May 8, 1875—I was in Keokuk, Iowa. I'd traveled back there to play a baseball game at the invitation of this boy's father." He lifted his hand toward Jack, who looked on with wide eyes, suddenly feeling like a million dollars in gold. John Dillon gave him a wink. "His name was Packy Dillon, my younger brother, a boy I had to leave behind when I fled for my life in the summer of '55."

The men appeared not to have been expecting a talk of this

sort. They shifted nervously, casting sidelong glances at Jack and their skipper, who walked back and forth as he spoke.

"Packy had sent me a letter way out here. He was a member of the St. Louie Red Stockings, he wrote. A pro team just starting out. And that they had a game lined up against the Keokuk Westerns, in that town I once lived in. See, Packy had notions of me coming out to meet him and his cap'n and joining that St. Louie club. And from there, we would play pro baseball together."

John Dillon studied his shoes as he paced. "Well, when I got back there, he handed me a pair of white knickers and bright red knee-high socks." He stopped to laugh. "And then he said, 'Here's how I see it. I'll be catching, and you'll be playing first base. Two brothers batting in the number three and number four spots.'"

While he paused, Jack's newfound uncle forced a grin. "So I say, 'Who's hitting fourth?' And he says, 'Well, me, naturally.' And I just shook my head saying, 'Only till they find out how far I can send it.'"

The men rumbled out agreement.

The cap'n walked to a bench and sat, clasping his hands between his knees. "Imagine it, will you?" he wheezed out. "Here we were, two motherless, fatherless boys, born as property, sold as property, and worked as hard-beaten slaves, whipped from the day we could walk to the day we ran off, making plans such as that." He dropped his head. It seemed that whatever memory the big man had conjured up had overtaken his ability to speak.

Into the thick silence that followed, Jack said, "What happened next, Uncle John? I mean, in the game. Did they let you play?"

He nodded strongly. "Yes, son, yes they did. I went in for a couple innings and I got myself one at bat."

"How'd you do?" Jack prodded.

Uncle John grinned a toothy grin. "I let them see how far I could send it." His eyes lifted to the ceiling. "I sailed the ball over the head of the Keokuk left fielder. So far, so fast, he didn't even bother to look up or turn around. Just hung down his head and cried."

Everyone laughed. John Dillon laughed even harder, shaking tears from his eyes. "It was a thing of beauty, I tell you. Watched it roll all the way to the river."

Jack was loving this story. "So your first time up in professional ball, you got yourself a home run? That is astounding."

His uncle shook his head. "Well, no. Actually, it turned out not to be all that astound-ish. You see, I was so impressed with the flight of the ball, that I missed first base for watching it. Ran right by the bag, they told me, and I suppose I did. Anyhow, after I rounded all the bases, the Westerns brought the ball back, touched first, and I was called out."

"No fair!" Jack cried, bouncing off the floor.

"Oh, it was fair, son." His voice was even again. "Unfortunate, but fair. That's the beautiful thing about baseball. The fairness."

He looked off again, into the memory. "After the game, they all tried to talk me into joining the team. Skipper, too. But I had not come back to Keokuk to join the St. Louie Red Stockings.

Nor to simply play one last game with my brother. I wanted to get him to follow me out West, to join me in creating the greatest ball club in the land. But we both had our reasons for standing pat. He was set on returning to his wife and family, and I wished to go into the future, into a better land, with this fine game of baseball." He paused before adding, "And I never saw him again."

Long John Dillon sat erect, his chest drawing tunnel loads of air, his eyes clearing.

The men milled about, gazing off, giving him time to collect himself.

Jack stepped close to peer into the big man's eyes. "Uncle John? Anything else?"

Uncle John shook his head. "No, not really. It's just a bit of a special day for me, is all. May the eighth. Baseball moon. Sunday afternoon. And my brother's boy is here." That hit Jack squarely in the heart. He felt a shiver.

Then Uncle John reconsidered. "Well, one more thing, I suppose. Fact is, I named my saloon after the lesson I learned that day."

Now his usual wide grin lit his face. "Seriously, boys. Don't never bother to hit yourself a home run 'less you plan to touch 'em all."

The roar was bigger than it probably should have been. Back slapping. Shaking off jitters. But Jack understood. The men were eager now to get to the ball field, to shed the raw emotions of a story that had indeed touched each one of them.

They spread wide, gathered their loose gear, talked louder

than usual, and after taking one last good-luck gulp of root beer, they headed for the door.

With determination filling their eyes, the ball club strode out of the mountain and onto the trail. They made their way down the hill, straight into town, awaiting the cheers and applause of the local citizens.

Which never came.

Along the boardwalk ahead, hundreds of locals stood silently, lining both sides of Maine Street, watching the team approach with somber eyes.

Jack could no longer hear the band as he had only minutes before. Once the team turned the corner at the Touch 'Em All and headed for Freedom Field, Jack saw why.

In front of Tia Rosa's Cantina stood the drummer boys, their drumsticks at their sides. The brassmen waited with folded arms. Stretching across the road was a group of several dozen townsfolk, lined up, blocking the team's path to the game.

"We won't let you do it, John." It was Mr. Becket, standing in the middle of the street, in front of everyone. "This game is off."

Uncle John asked for no explanation. Standing under the *cantina*'s front-porch overhang, smirking and rocking on their heels, were Mr. Hulbert and Mr. Toots. Apparently, the townsfolk had been informed of the true stakes of the game.

"You can't quit, Dillon," yelled Hulbert, striding out into the street, "just because your little chicken-scratch town here doesn't have the stomach for it. You ought to tell them, walking away won't let you off the hook."

"John," Mr. Becket interceded. "We read the papers you signed. If you play this game, we either lose the town or we lose the team to Cincinnati. But if there's no game, there's no bet. No one prevails."

"Do you forfeit the contest?" asked Mr. Hulbert.

Long John Dillon raised his arms. "Now hold on, everyone. Mr. Becket, if I go back on my word now, I might as well lay down right here and die. For I will have no honor left."

Now others in the crowd joined in. "You should've thought of that before," called one fellow.

Uncle John turned to face the man. "Sir, there is never a moment in my day when I do not think about my honor. And I intend to stand by my word. Now let us pass."

Several more men rushed forward to stop him. "No, sir. No game today." Others jeered at him. "You lost your honor when you entered into this deal!" came a call. "You don't run this entire town, you know," came another. "We got rights."

Uncle John roared back. "Gentlemen! Do not try to stop me." He turned to face the onlookers lining the street. "Listen to me. All of you."

The crowd fell silent.

"During my first year out here, I saw a countryside full of Indians, Mexicans, blacks, whites, and Chinese. Working, living together. And for the first time in my life, I felt proud to be a part of this land." He studied their faces. "Way out here in this little corner of the world, all men were equal. So I built my ballpark. And I built this town around that ball field and that principle.

Now we either go forward, or I have no choice but to sign the mine over to Mr. Hulbert, here and now."

The closest man yelled, "You're a fool, Dillon."

"Maybe so, but right now this fool is offering you the only chance we still have to keep this town around. The way we like it. And give it a second life."

Without waiting for a response, he turned toward the team. "Men, let's go." He began to march, to lead the ball club through the crowd, toward the field. The crowd parted, slowly, with fire still in the eyes of many.

Jack saw Mr. Hulbert laughing, as if he and Mr. Toots knew something no one else did.

But as the team stepped past the last of the human roadblock, one boy on the streetside, about Jack's age, yelled, "I ain't a-chicken of those Chicago boys, Cap'n. Who do they think they are? Go get 'em! You're gonna win, win, win!"

Like a trickle of water over a dike, that one small voice started a flood of calls.

"All my money's on you, boys!" yelled one man.

"Send those city slickers back across the desert where they belong!" shouted another.

Through the boasts and hoots that built like thunderclouds, the Dillontown Nine walked silently. Focused and serious, their metal cleats sending up chunks of earth, they stepped to the beat of the big bass drum.

Boom-lay, boom-lay, boom-lay, boom.

One o'clock, Sunday. Game time. The grandstands
were packed. The entire field was lined with people, standing ten
or fifteen deep. It seemed the whole town had emptied, some
fifteen hundred people, to witness the historic match.

Everyone was there. Everyone except Billy.

Horse carriages lined the roadways and filled the meadows.
Picnic baskets and colorful blankets lay scattered around the
outskirts of the field, under trees, and on the boulders nearby.
The telegraph wires must have been buzzing all night.

Eliza stood near the team dugout surrounded by a group
of the most ardent Dillontown supporters, telling them a story of
last night's adventure, one that Jack admired with all his heart.

"*Ay, sí,* he rode off upon a white stallion, the finest horse in
our stable. I struggle and I fight with him, but I had to give the
horse to Billy the Kid, or I would die!"

At this point, the exquisite actress placed her hands around
her neck in a choking hold, opened her mouth, and crossed her
eyes, looking very much like an exquisite corpse.

Meanwhile, along the edges of the outfield, a loose chain of
boys and girls played a game of their own. They tossed several

red cloth balls in one direction while a blue denim ball slowly made its way along the chain from the other. The trick seemed to be to keep from getting conked from behind by the blue ball while catching and tossing the red ones down the line.

The Dillontown Brass Band, dressed in red shirts and blue pants, with gold stripes down the sides, marched around the inside perimeter of the field several times, stirring up the crowd with boom-lay-booms and root-a-toot toots. On the second time around, they paused in center field, just below the rising moon, as the team officials were called together to meet at the pitcher's box for the coin toss.

For some strange reason, Cap Anson, the player-manager of the White Stockings, was not present. Jack had heard a rumor that Anson, one of the most heralded ballplayers in America, was miffed at having to play against a team he considered "beneath him." So in his absence, Silver Flint, the team's catcher, represented the Chicagoans, calling, "Heads."

The coin came up tails. And though Uncle John had toyed with the idea of choosing to have the hometown nine bat first—to get a demoralizing jump on the White Stockings—Barnaby, the umpire, let the crowd know that "The home team, which will occupy the first-base dugout, wins the toss, choosing to take the field first and bat last."

That caused a whoop, and the band started up again to continue its rounds.

Jack warmed up with the rest of the team in their brand-new uniforms, fresh off yesterday's stage. His shirt was so huge, he could carry his bat across his shoulders just by stabbing it through his sleeves, and it still wouldn't affect his ability to throw. Of course, nothing could faze him today. Here he was, standing amongst the tobacco-chewing, whisker-chin-drooling, cuss-word-spewing brigade, while having a toss with Rico Del Rey from Havana, Cuba, and floating two feet off the ground.

Every time Dixie Bodine would glance over at Jack, he'd say something like, "Kee-rye-miny sakes! Lookee here. This boy's skinnier than a cornstalk and twice as green." Once, he spat out a long stream of hacked black tobacco juice, which landed on Jack's shoe, saying, "Careful I don't grab you by the ankles, son, and use you for a bat. I been known to do worse."

Jack wished with all his heart that Billy could be there, just to hear Jack wonder out loud, "Am I in heaven, son, or am I only dreaming?"

After Uncle John's call for the team to head in, Rico fired one last toss, which Jack caught with a healthy snap, one that brought him right back down to earth. He said nothing, but since he'd been briefly distracted and failed to watch the ball all the way, he'd caught it on a tender part of his left hand, just below the pinky finger, the same finger he'd hurt during his two high-speed dismounts the day he met Billy. Only this time he heard a tiny crack.

Had he been wearing a glove, it probably would not have happened. But in all the games he'd played up until this one, only catchers and first basemen wore gloves. Today, however, he saw that he was the only player on the field who did not sport a glove.

Without looking, Jack immediately placed his left hand under his right arm and walked toward the dugout, telling himself, "It's gonna be fine. It's gonna be fine."

Over the top of the mountain wall, a desert wind began drifting in. A gust or two rustled the banners hung from the stands. Just a gust or two.

"Boys, listen up." Long John Dillon strode toward the bench and peered down from the field.

"They're tossing Corcoran today, as expected. Now, he may be a little fellow, but he's a double-barrel shooter. He can come at you right-handed or left-handed, anytime he wants. Good fastball, either way, so read the spin. A first-rate roundhouse curve from the left side, so read the spin. And a drop ball each way that'll get you every time if you don't do what?"

"Read the *spin!*" yelled everyone, with fists shaking.

"That's right. Just remember, your purpose at that white stone today is to corrupt that doggone baseball like you're slapping chicken eggs with a shovel."

The men rocked and rumbled their agreement.

"Where's Anson?" asked Dixie, eyeing the field. "I heard he's not playing."

"I heard he was too good for us," said Jésus.

Uncle John turned around to scout the field himself, and just as he did, Cap Anson strolled into the park, escorted by none other than Mr. Hulbert himself. "There's your answer, boys. Don't believe everything you hear."

Jack watched the tall first sacker step down into the Chicago dugout and noticed that not a single teammate greeted him.

Uncle John spun back and proceeded to call out the list of

starters for the day's game, putting LaFay at second, Buckles in left, and moving Jésus to short. That left Jack on the pine along with the veteran reliever Lefty Wright.

"Now, go out there and play some ball!" cried Uncle John.

When the gong sounded to start the match, the bench emptied and the stands roared at the sight of the home rubes dashing forth in their spanking blue and white togs. At the top of the steps, Dixie shed the old gray wool sweater he'd draped over his "whippin' wing," slung it to the bench, and trotted out.

In contrast, the White Stockings wore the reverse of any ball club Jack had ever seen. Pure black uniforms from the cap on down, except for their wide white belts and long white socks, nearly up to their knees. They conjured up the image of a ruthless band of outlaws working for a desperado king.

The umpire shouted, "Play!"

"Cal McVey," cried the announcer as Chicago's first batter, a sawed-off, bull-chested man, taut with muscles from his ankles to his jaw, strode forth.

"Put one on the platter," he called to the pitcher. "I don't aim to stand up here too long."

"Would three pitches be long enough?" came Dixie's reply, followed by a juicy stream of tobacco, ten feet long, with a little extra running down his chin.

"Only if you want to waste two of 'em." McVey spat on the handle of his bat, squirmed both hands against it, then dug in.

The first pitch sailed at McVey's head.

He dropped to one knee, casual as a man tying his shoe, letting it pass over top, as if he hardly noticed. Then he gazed absently toward the field, the way a fisherman might scout a lake.

"Get back up there," yelled Dixie. "I got a closer one."

McVey was not fazed, however. He timed the next pitch perfectly and hammered a low screaming liner just to the left of Jésus. The shortstop ran and lunged for it, snagging the ball in the air by his fingertips for the first out.

"They came to hit," said Jack.

Lefty nodded. "They came to win."

But for that inning at least, the hitting never came. The next batter popped up to LaFay at second, and Tonio ran under a foul pop-up by King Kelly behind third for out number three.

"Boy," said Jack, "Dixie's pitching is sure something. That ball jumped and humped all the way home." He used his hand to trace out a camel's back.

"Tough to hit," Lefty agreed as he rose with Dixie's sweater in his hand. He met the crafty hurler outside the dugout and helped him slide on the right arm, to keep his shoulder warm.

Jésus led off for the Dillontowners with a high fly ball to left for the first out. When Tonio popped out to shortstop, it looked as though a pitcher's duel was brewing. But Corcoran was cautious with Long John Dillon, now batting third in place of Shadowfox Coe. After starting him off with a right-handed fastball, which the cap'n hammered down the left-field line—but foul—he switched to his other arm. However, not being fully warmed with his southpaw, Corcoran threw seven straight balls, high and low, and Long John trotted to first base with a walk.

Blackjack Buck came to the home stone, and Rico slapped

Jack's knee and lifted his chin toward the husky batter. "Watch this. I got a feeling."

It didn't take long for Rico's feeling to spread through the park. Blackjack Buck, a lefty, drove the first pitch he saw deep over the head of King Kelly in right field. Even with Kelly's famous speed, he would not catch up to this shooting star.

"Hew-ta!" yelled Jack, bouncing off the bench.

"I told you," said Rico, clapping and shouting.

And though Fence Post followed with a pop-up to Quest on a dipsy-doodle pitch, the Dillontown Nine went into the second inning leading two to nothing.

George Gore led off for Chicago, timing Dixie's third pitch well enough to hit a deep fly to Fence Post in center, but the sure-handed outfielder ran under it for out number one.

Next, the already-legendary Cap Anson, who now had a swagger about him, sauntered up to the home stone. The oldest member of the Chicago team, Anson was also their wiliest player.

Dixie, however, was less than impressed. He used his drop ball to retire Anson on a grounder to Tonio at third. It was not a close play, but for some reason Anson continued to run at full speed and barely missed stomping on Uncle John's foot as he brushed past, crossing the base.

"What's the big fat idea?" said Jack, rising to his feet. "Is he trying to hurt someone?" From the first-base dugout, Jack had a perfect view. He could also hear Anson spout off as he ran past Uncle John on his return.

"You're a dern fool to put your mine up, boy. I'm only playing to make sure you don't have a cotton-pickin' chance of winning this game." Luckily for him, he kept on running, because Uncle John had coal fires burning in his eyes.

Chicago's shortstop, Tom Burns, fared no better at bat, ending the inning on a chopper to Jésus at short.

"Let's tack some more on," called John Dillon, running in from first. "And, boys, be wary of that big goon, Anson. He's a mean sack of chitlins."

"Don't worry, Cap'n," said Dixie. "I know his type. He won't be flappin' them lips with a fastball flying down his word hole."

Rico began the second inning with a walk, which brought up Mr. Jim Buckles, the new man who proved out to be a bit rocky. A strong batsman, sure, but the first time up, every swing he took, he put his foot in the bucket, as if he were getting ready to run to third to get out of the way of Corcoran's sidearm sling pitch.

"Stay in the box and bat!" John Dillon yelled. "Or I'll stake that front foot of yours to the ground."

Well, that just seemed to upset the man. He commenced to sit on the next eight pitches and finally drew a walk, to put runners on first and second.

Mr. Tom LaFay, Dillontown's number eight hitter, had no clue what to do against Corcoran's slingshot either. Or his roundhouse. So with two runners on board, he merely stuck out his wagon-tongue bat and swatted a lucky looper to center field. It fell in, though, loading up the bases.

Just when it looked like something was cooking, Dixie got fooled on a "dang-blasted change-a-pace," grounding the ball right back to Corcoran, who had no trouble scooping it to Silver Flint at home to get Del Rey. Flint, in turn, fired the ball to first base to make a double play on poor Dixie, who was still chugging down the line.

The entire team huddled at the far corner of the dugout when Dixie returned. No telling where his bat would be flying off to.

But Jésus saved the day when he chopped down hard on the ball and drove a bounding single into right field. Two more runs crossed the plate.

The crowd burst into bellows, boom-lays, and bullet blasts. It came so loud and sudden, Jack likened the sound to a thunderstorm inside a house.

Tonio grounded out to end the inning, but now the home boys had a four to nothing lead, and it seemed to them to be just another day of business as usual.

The score stayed that way until the fifth, when Cal McVey homered for the White Stockings, but even at four to one, the Dillontowners walked with an air of confidence.

Then the winds began to blow. What had been at first a few gusts now became a constant breeze out of the east and into the batter's face.

It hardly fazed the White Stockings, though. In fact, the breeze seemed to wake them up. Silver Flint started off the sixth with a home run to left center. And by the time George Gore drove a screaming three-run homer down the right-field line, the White Stockings had taken the lead, five to four.

Neither team scored in the seventh, but even so, the pressure of this high-stakes game had just about frozen LaFay, who could not bring himself to even swing the bat anymore. Having embarrassed himself at the home stone all day, he'd taken to sipping tonic from Little Lou Montague's medicine jug to "heal the fierce pain in my shoulder bone," or so he claimed. But after being called out on strikes in the seventh, the poor man wandered off, woozy, and fell asleep on a pile of stones out past the grandstands.

Uncle John stared at Lefty Wright, but said nothing. He paced around the first-base coacher's box, calling orders and clapping his hands, but gave no indication as to how he was going to solve his infield problem.

Jack decided to use every measure of silent persuasion he could think of to influence that decision.

Lefty stood up and began to stretch. The inning ended. Uncle John approached. "Jack, why don't you go on out to second base. Can't do no worse than that poor boy."

And that was it. Jack only had to uncross his legs, uncross his arms and his fingers and his eyes, then tumble off the bench and dash out to the infield for the next big dream of his life to become a reality.

It may have been the top of the eighth, he may have had a broken left hand, and his team might be losing, five to four, but at long last, he was playing for the Dillontown Nine.

Big storm rising," said Rico, heading out to right field at the start of the eighth.

Jack looked east as he took the field himself. Over the mountain ridge, he saw tall dark clouds billowing up.

"Looks like thunderclouds is all," said Jack. "I don't see any rain. Don't they usually blow apart over the hills?" He had seen the pattern many times as a young boy.

Rico ran backward to answer. "Not when the east wind blows. Then those clouds usually cross all the way over. And they have rain."

Jack felt the warm desert wind hit his face. "Well, then, we'll just have to win this thing before the storm gets here."

The wind seemed to be helping Dixie—at first. In the top of the eighth, his dipsy-do was unhittable. But then, as the wind gusted up, he lost control of it. With one out in the eighth, King Kelly drew a walk.

"Watch for the steal," yelled Jack. "Be ready, boys."

Next, the mighty George Gore, the man who had already laced a homer into the crowd, stood in.

"Go get 'im, Dixie!" cried Uncle John.

"Darn tootin'!" said Jack.

And Dixie did his best. All Gore could do on a slicing slip-and-dip pitch was to hit a one-bounce sky-hopper to first base.

Jack sprinted behind Uncle John to back him up, but he could see that the Dillontown cap'n had the play under control. He could also see that the ball was hanging up longer than he'd expected, and that as soon as it came down, there would be a leg race to the bag between Uncle John and Gore.

Barnaby the umpire darted down the line as well, so he could get a better view.

Uncle John clapped onto the bounder, then dashed to his base.

"Run, Uncle John, run!" Jack dropped down on one knee to watch.

George Gore, a great runner himself, bore down with all his might. Lunging with a giant step, he reached the canvas bag an instant before the first baseman's foot.

"Safe!" cried Barnaby, skidding up behind him with one hand holding his hat to his head.

Being the alert baseball man he was, John Dillon quickly spun around and looked to see what Kelly was up to on second base.

No need. Kelly wasn't there. He stood at third.

A racehorse could not have covered that amount of ground in the few seconds the play had lasted. Nor had Kelly. For it turned out that King Kelly had truly "stolen" second base. Stolen right past it, that is.

Dixie jumped up and down in the pitcher's box, pointing at the culprit. "He cut across the infield!"

Jésus yelled, pounding his fist. "The runner, he never touched second base!"

The crowd was in an uproar, too, screaming, jeering, whistling, and stomping their feet.

It appeared to Jack that once Kelly had seen the umpire run up the line, he'd hightailed it directly across the diamond.

Barnaby looked at Jésus. Then he rested his eyes on Kelly. Finally, he said, "I didn't see it. If I didn't see it, I can't call it."

"But we're telling you!" said Dixie.

"And," Barnaby said, "I'm telling *you*. Batter is safe at first. Runner is safe at third. Now play!"

The whole team fumed and grumbled some more, but Barnaby's decision would stand.

Kelly only shrugged, a picture of innocence, as if he couldn't understand what all the fuss was about.

Sadly, it hardly mattered. After Anson singled and Burns doubled a moment later, not only had Kelly scored, but the White Stockings would take a three-run lead into the bottom of the eighth inning. They now led seven to four.

Dixie, who had not shown himself to be a strong hitter, slipped Jack's iron bat into his hands for the first time that day and got set to lead off the bottom of the eighth.

"Shoot, I might just walk up there with this boy's lucky horseshoe bat and send that ball to Rattlesnake Ridge." He didn't, but when he did pick up his own stick, the difference was obvious.

"That's the way to whip that willow," said Fence Post, admiring the swing of the old Arkansan. "Go get 'er, Dix."

That put a little hop in the lanky man's step, and on the second pitch, Dixie reached out and laced a low line drive over the head of the second baseman and into right center. The hit fired everyone up.

"Now you go get 'em, Jésus," cried Lefty. "If that old man can do it, you can, too."

Jésus answered with a sharp grounder to short, which appeared to be a perfect double-play ball until it hit a stone in the base path and took a wicked hop—right into the throat of the shortstop, Tom Burns.

By the time the third baseman, McVey, gathered the ball, there were runners at first and second with no outs. And Burns lay writhing on the ground, his hands around his neck, as he tried to catch his breath.

Everybody in the park seemed to hold their breath, too.

Finally, in the midst of his teammates, the man settled, lying quiet for a bit. A few moments later, under orders from Cap Anson, they carted Burns off the field. He was simply too bruised and shaken to go on. Second sacker Joe Quest took his spot while McVey shuffled from third to second, and Ned Williamson came off the bench to replace McVey at third.

Though it was hard to see any man go down, all the role-shifting the White Stockings had to go through was seen as a break for the Dillontown Nine.

"We got 'em all mixed up," said Fence Post. "What say we drive each one of 'em off the field and back to where they came from?"

Tonio did what he could, singling to left field and sending Jésus to second while Dixie Bodine crossed the stone with Dillontown's fifth run.

Now with men on first and second, and his team down by two runs, Long John Dillon did something that will stay in the minds of baseball enthusiasts forever. He had thought and thought on it, he later said. Ever since he'd seen the new rube, LaFay, stab his bat at the ball, he'd turned the idea over and over in his head.

As soon as Corcoran ran up and hurled his pitch, Uncle John stood to face him, holding the bat parallel to the ground. Yes, he was bunting, which was surprising enough, but he never intended for it to be a base hit. He had another purpose in mind.

"Baby hit!" called Anson, using the sneer term the old-timers hung on the newfangled bunt. The slapped ball rolled down the third-base line, and by the time Williamson had gloved it, his only play was to first base. Just as Long John had planned.

Not exactly a RIM play, it was instead the world's first sacrifice bunt. Uncle John's whole intent had been to move the runners along and into scoring position, whether he made it to first base or not. Jack couldn't believe he hadn't thought of the trick himself. But he hooted just the same.

Runners now stood on second and third, with only one out. Blackjack Buck—representing the go-ahead run—strolled to the hitter's box.

Corcoran greeted him with two quick called strikes, low and away. The next pitch, though, shot inside, right in Buck's wheelhouse, and he offered a mighty cut. The ball flew a mile high. Jack bolted out of the dugout to watch its flight, willing it to fly on. But the ball made it only to shallow right field. The wind had caught it and held it. In fact, King Kelly had to trot in a few steps as the ball fell harmlessly into his hands. Two outs. And no one had scored.

Uncle John, now standing once again in the first-base coacher's box, clapped his hands. "Up to you, Hayes!"

Fence Post clutched his hand-whittled four-by-four and tapped it on the stone.

"Is that all you can do, boy?" Anson yelled to Uncle John. "Go up and get your baby-slap roller and let the real men on your team do the work?"

Anson knew what every player knew. That if Uncle John took

his bait and started a fight, he'd be thrown out of the game, desperately hurting Dillontown's chances.

Still, it looked for a moment as if Long John Dillon was considering a Long John killin'. He glared at Anson, then spat.

Anson's face grew a fiery red. "You think you're something, don't you? You're nothing. Mark my words, no matter what happens today, you will never play one game in the National League. None of your kind will. And that's no threat. That's a promise."

As if forcing himself to ignore the man, Uncle John slowly turned, squaring his shoulders toward the home stone.

Corcoran delivered, and Fence Post drove the ball hard on the ground toward Anson at first, almost as if the feisty slugger had planned to knock the ball down the man's throat. Instead, Anson knocked it down, shuffled off to retrieve it, then dashed for the bag. But Fence Post legged it out, beating Anson to the base for a single. Meanwhile, Jésus trotted home with the second run of the inning.

The Dillontowners were battling back, down now by only one, seven to six.

Long John Dillon said nothing, as was his manner, but the whole Dillontown dugout hooted at Anson—no one could resist—suggesting that it was time for an old crow like him to hang up his spikes before he crippled himself and became the laughingstock of baseball.

Anson's face only burnt darker red as he spat into his glove.

With runners at first and third, up stepped Rico.

A hawk flew overhead. *"Kee-kee,"* it cried, lazily riding a thermal updraft as it circled the park.

The winds had changed again, the bird seemed to be saying. Now the warm air was rising.

And the next thing to ride a thermal updraft was the fly ball Rico launched into deep left field for a stupendous home run— as if that old red-tailed hawk had directed him to do it. The pandemonium that followed, after Rico's whack added three more runs to the board, however, was all his doing.

How could they lose now? thought Jack as he joined his teammates in whooping and slapping the Havana boy's back. How could they lose now?

With their club out in front, nine to seven, the home crowd was hoppin', stompin', and knockin' each other left, right, up, and down. On the Cuban's three-run round-tripper, the whole game had turned around.

Buckles, the eighth man to bat in the inning, finally got good wood on the ball himself, sending another blast into the sky. But Abner Dalrymple, the Chicago left fielder, managed to run it down for the third out.

Even so, the Dillontowners took the field in the top of the ninth, having scored five runs in their at bat and gained a two-run lead.

"We're just about home free," called Fence Post.

"We ain't nowhere yet," said Long John Dillon. "We got three outs to go. Now, let's hold 'em."

Uncle John was right to be cautious, and Jack knew it. After all, this was a national championship team they were up against.

Leadoff man Cal McVey proved it by opening the top of the ninth with a single to left center. He moved to second on a single to right by Quest.

Now King Kelly stood at the stone.

Jack's heart sank. He could see the whole game starting to slip away. He backed up a step, flexing his sore hand, bracing for a possible heater of a ground ball off Kelly's bat.

But Dixie's fastball was the heater. As the mighty Kelly lowered his stick to go down and get it, he misjudged it by a tick, sending a high pop fly into foul territory behind home. Blackjack Buck tracked it and squeezed it into his shiny new mitt. No damage. No runs.

Not yet, leastways.

"Just two more outs, Dixie," shouted Jack. He glanced around the infield. "How about a double play, boys?"

That was a lot to ask with speedy George Gore at the plate. Besides, he seemed to have another idea. He jumped on a dipsy-do pitch that dipsy-didn't, and blasted a single to right center, driving in McVey and bringing Joe Quest to third with the tying run.

Uncle John pounded his fist into his glove. "Bear down, Dixie! We gotta stop 'em right here."

Cap Anson, the spiteful man who had been riding Uncle John all day, walked to the stone. And as if it were an answer to Jack's silent request, Anson swatted a perfect one-hop double-play grounder to Uncle John at first, who fielded it right at the bag.

Ah, how sweet, thought Jack. *This* was the *perfect* way to end the match.

Once Uncle John tapped first, he spun and whipped the ball to Jésus, who was standing on second. Jésus simply had to lay down the tag on Gore, and the game would be over.

And Anson would be the goat. Perfect.

But on his way to second, Gore must've realized he could not possibly beat the throw. So he stopped halfway as the ball sailed past his head—and turned around! His only chance of keeping the game alive was to head back to first. This was perfectly legal, since Uncle John had already gotten the out at first, so Gore was no longer forced to advance.

"He's going back to first!" yelled Jack, only a few feet from Jésus. "Throw it! Throw it!"

Jésus never paused. He caught the ball and threw it right back to Uncle John, who stretched out and caught it belt high, down on one knee to slap the tag on Gore. But the tag was too late.

George Gore had made a brilliant play. For not only did he slide safely back into first, but as he did, Joe Quest had darted home from third to tie the game, nine to nine.

The whole park fell quiet. Shocked. The only sounds were a few scattered cheers and Cap Anson's cackling laugh.

The next batter, Williamson, hit a soft grounder to Jack at second, who flipped the ball to Uncle John for the final out, but the damage was done. And the barrage of language spewing from Anson at that point—even with women present—was worse than Jack had ever heard.

Amongst other things, Anson was utterly gleeful that this "fat field slave" didn't have "the brains of a dumb monkey" to foresee Gore's split-second read and reaction to a complicated play. "You deserve to lose, boy!" he yelled.

"This is California," Dixie said to Uncle John. "You know you don't have to take that venom."

Uncle John stared straight ahead. Slowly he said, "There will be a time and a place. And this ain't neither." His voice rose. "Boys, it's up to us to end this thing right now! Bottom of the ninth. Let's go!"

Jack Dillon, Dixie Bodine, and Jésus de Luz were due up. And if any of them got on board, Tonio Wingo, John Dillon, or Blackjack Buck were ready to drive them home and drive the home boys all the way to Cincinnati.

What a perfect moment, thought Jack, to make my rookie hitting debut. Except that he was barely able to grip the bat. He bit his lip against the pain stabbing into his left palm. He swung as hard as he could at the very first pitch he saw, but missed it completely. With his hand in its current condition, he had lost almost all control of the bat. Two more butterfly pitches, and he was gone. Jack's throbbing hand felt like a boulder had rolled over it.

Dixie came up next and battled hard, but was finally defeated on strikes as well. Now the game rested on the shoulders of Jésus.

And Jésus squared those shoulders, laying down a perfect bunt. Slapped onto the grass halfway between the pitcher and first base, it was a holy roller only the second baseman could field.

McVey hustled in and grabbed it on the run, but never bothered to throw. Jésus was safe by a country mile. Jack stood in awe of that bunt. It was the opposite of a HEW-TA hit. In fact, Jésus hit it right at McVey, only it died on the way out. What a touch.

Then Jésus did something only two men on the field happened to notice, Tonio and Jack. As Tonio Wingo made his way to the home stone, Jésus caught his attention by saying, *"Kee-kee,"* the cry of the hawk. But he had more to say. He touched his cap. The rim of his cap. That is, as they both explained later, the *RIM* of his cap.

He sent Tonio a signal that they had worked out in advance—that he was ready to steal, and that Tonio should be ready to hit the next pitch no matter where it was, and, preferably, "where they ain't."

As soon as he saw Jésus begin his steal, second baseman McVey left his spot to cover his base.

Tonio saw that and slapped a grounder right through the hole and into right field. What a play! Two men on, two out. And up stepped John Dillon.

Now, in these parts, folks say that baseball is heaven's game. Descended from the ancient Native American stick-and-ball game known by some as lacrosse, it's been played in some version by hundreds of tribes, including the Hopi, the Apache, and the Quechan, for centuries upon centuries, both for reasons of conflict resolution and "as a way to give thanks to the Creator."

Jack definitely thought baseball had angels involved. In fact, he knew there were. Why else would he have been guided to Dillontown?

But the angels must have been working overtime that afternoon, to place Long John Dillon in this spot, at this moment, on this day. With Cap Anson watching.

Uncle John stepped to the stone. The big right-hander waved

his club over it, taking the measure of his swing. He twisted his metal cleats into the soft, moist earth, snugging first his back foot, then the front.

Corcoran delivered. High.

The ritual was repeated. This time the ball clipped the outside edge of the strike zone. But it was not to Uncle John's liking. Ball one, strike one.

Jack mumbled a few words skyward. Every Dillontown player stood on the top step of the dugout, breathing their own talismanic words, making their own sacred signs.

The set. The run-up. The pitch.

Chest high, over the plate. And Uncle John got it all. A towering blast, high into center field, heading for the moon—at least to the spot where the moon had been before the clouds had blown in.

Into the wind, the eastern wind, it flew. Rising higher. Then it hung, it wafted, it stalled. And into the open hands of galloping George Gore, it fell. Three outs.

That ain't right, thought Jack. That's not how it was supposed to be.

Still, he realized, it was not over. The score was nine to nine. And the tenth inning was about to begin.

Extra innings! thought Jack. I still get to play, and we still have a chance.

Reinspired, he sprang from the dugout and ran out to second base so quickly, the Chicago second sacker, Cal McVey, was still walking in from shallow right field. McVey tossed Jack his fingerless leather mitt. "Here you go, kid. Give it a try." He winked. "But don't get me out."

"Thank you, sir." If a big strong man like McVey could wear padding on his hand at second base, Jack figured he could, too. He pulled the sweaty-palmed glove onto his left hand. Halfway. He could not get it past his bottom knuckles. Small glove? No, his hand was that swollen. His palm had nearly doubled in size.

He tried to bend it. His hand was stiff as an old saddle. Huge raindrops began to fall, but he scarcely noticed. He explored his swollen hand with the other, and all he found was sharp knife-blade pain. More drops fell. And more, plopping onto the dirt baseline, raising small puffs of dust. Soon the dust had gone to mud, with a downpour that sounded like a drummer's roll.

The storm had come after all.

"Hey, kid!" called Fence Post. "How much sense were you born with?"

Jack was the only player on the field. Pretending the fast-flying storm had simply mesmerized him, he looked up.

"I think it'll pass!" he shouted back, though he doubted anyone could hear with the rain pounding so hard, not to mention the thunder that followed.

Spectators crossed the ball yard in swarms, and as many as could fit ducked under the grandstand canopy. There they stood, like spooked cattle, milling, looking out into the deluge with glassy eyes.

The rest of the folks relied on hats and parasols and tugged-up shirts—save the practical-minded few who traipsed off toward the dry shelter of the nearest saloon.

Slowly Jack trudged into the dugout. Rain or shine, he knew one thing. There would be no more baseball for him. Red meat, he decided. I need some red meat to slap on this hand.

Barnaby, still behind the home stone, waved his arms. "Managers!" he shouted. Both managers came out and huddled with the umpire to discuss the situation.

At first, Barnaby said he would give the storm a half hour before he would either postpone the match or officially call the game a tie. However, since the White Stockings had a boat to catch on Monday and needed to leave town first thing in the morning, no one wanted that. Including Barnaby.

"I'll be back in thirty minutes to assess the situation," he said. "If things are looking better, then I'll give it another little while for the storm to pass. Best I can do, boys." Barnaby tipped his hat, sending rainwater sloshing off the flat top and brim, then strolled away.

Every baseball game is the story of a lifetime.

On the first pitch, you are born. The battle begins.

For nine long innings, you struggle. You make some good plays, you make errors. You take or you swing. You hit or sit. But even he who hits 'em where they ain't cannot stop the wind or rain.

Your team becomes your family, your circle, the calmers of your soul. Even the orphan feels at home. For though you may run onto the ball field together, you must face the fastball alone.

When the game ends, you either had a good life or a bad one or a hobgoblin of both. But it's over, right? You move on. Take whatever you have gathered and go. Because tomorrow—and here's the best part—tomorrow, you are born again.

Jack burst into the cathedral room with his horseshoe bat in one hand and a slice of Tia Rosa's beef wrapped up around the other.

"Billy, they stopped the game because of rain. It's tied in the tenth. We need you. I can't play. My hand's too sore. One of those new boys was a washout, and the other one stinks. So you have to take over for me. Here, take the bat. You have to loosen up."

Billy sat thoughtfully in one of the red thrones, turned to face the center of the room. "You're wacky, aren't you?"

"I am, son, but what's your point?" Jack smiled in glee.

Billy did not seem to appreciate Jack's splendid impersonation of him.

"I was hoping I'd get to lie low one more day," said Billy, "until that marshal's on down the line."

"He's gone, I tell you. He had a string of boys out looking for you, but they all came back wet and grumpy." And if that wasn't precisely true, well, Jack figured it should've been. He went on. "Meantime, Eliza's got everyone convinced you're far across the border by now. On a white horse. She is a stellar actress, by the way."

Billy ignored that, too. "I can't do it, son. Look, I'd be a sitting duck out there, for anyone with a notion. You know that. Besides, as much as I'd like to help, I'm no ballplayer."

"So what? You're a fighter, aren't you? And this team needs your fight. And your talents. And with the ball club standing all around you, no one's gonna come gunning for you. We'll see to that."

What Jack failed to mention was that half the town regarded Billy as a kidnapper and a *desperado loco* who'd put a girl's life ahead of his own. Ah, but first things first. "What do you say, Bill Henry?"

Billy stared intently at Jack's meat hand. "How'd you do that?"

Scenes of diving for line drives, snagging red-hot grounders, flashed through Jack's thought box. But he deflected them all for the nearest thing he could possibly say without actually parting with the truth.

"I injured it so my best friend would get a chance to play."

"You lying pile of chicken bones."

Jack did not battle the matter. He had a war to win. "Let me see the soles of your boots."

"What for?"

Jack dropped to his knees to inspect Billy's shoe leather.

"Too slick," he proclaimed.

"They're just fine. Put my foot down."

Jack obliged. He rose and hustled to the small dirt wall where, because of a certain barrage of bullets the previous night, a smooth layer of fresh dirt had collected as the impacts had sent clump after clump sliding down.

He sifted through the dirt and spied a chunk of quartz crystal.

"Perfect," he said.

Running back to where Billy sat, he said, "Let me scuff up your soles some. You'll need the traction out on the ball field."

Billy drew his feet close. "Leave my boots alone. You *are* wacky, aren't you?"

Jack rested back on his haunches, gazing up at Billy, calculating. Deciding he needed to use an emotional tug like he'd never used before, he held out the rock for Billy to see, then closed his hand around it.

"Fine," he said. "I won't scratch up your boots. But, look, we *are* in a tough, tough spot. We need you, brother Billy. We just really do."

The outlaw took in a full breath, eyeing Jack strongly as he let it out.

With his arms folded hard against his chest, he rocked forward, parting his lips into that bucktooth grin of his. Then this accidental ballplayer stood up and said, "What do you want me to do?"

The downpour lasted nearly forty-five minutes before the sun broke through, and a window of time seemed to open up, at least for a little while, to restart the game.

Storm clouds still loomed to the east. And Jack still loomed in the game. He had to. The moment Uncle John saw Billy, he booted Buckles from the squad and put Billy in his spot.

"Desperate times," said the cap'n, "call for desperado measures."

Those measures were also taken by Billy, who of course wore a uniform, but still he hung his gun belt on a nail in the dugout—for easy access.

The uproar, though, that cascaded down when the crowd caught sight of Billy running out onto the field threatened to halt the game faster than any thunderstorm.

"He's a stone-cold killer!" a man yelled. "He nearly killed Eliza."

"He's a *murderer*!" cried another. "Stop him."

"Shoot him!" came the next cry. "He's a walking gold mine!"

Long John Dillon did not hesitate. He swooped down upon

Billy, with both arms raised, the way an eagle will dance around a chick with a pack of coyotes closing in.

"Yes, folks, I know," Uncle John boomed in his baritone voice. "This here is Billy the Kid. But there are two sides to every story."

"We know all about him and his story, Dillon." A raucous bunch of miners, with anger in their bellies and dollar signs in their eyes, stood facing Uncle John.

"No, you don't. I'm here to tell you, Eliza de Luz was in no more danger in this man's hold than she was with a crazy marshal waving his gun at her."

Now a hush began to fall.

And with a gallant grace, Uncle John began pacing the shortstop ground like a gladiator in the center of an arena, addressing the entire circle of people.

"This boy, Bill Henry Bonney, was promised his freedom and a full pardon by Governor Lew Wallace of New Mexico, who then broke his promise. This young fella should be a free man now." He let those words echo around the ballpark and against the mountains to the east.

"Billy the Kid is a friend of mine." He took a moment to face Billy, exchange nods with him, then go on. "He is a friend of this team, and he was willing to put his life on the line to walk onto this field to help this town. To help all of you." A murmur of sympathy seemed to ripple through the ballpark with that comment. But then Uncle John topped it.

"If you choose to shoot him, you will have to shoot me first.

For I shall put my life on the line for any man who has done so for me and my town."

His cool dark eyes painted over the entire field as he circled in place. Satisfied he had no challengers, he lowered his head and started for his position at first base, taking long, certain strides.

The crowd went wild. The "gunshot chorus" who had shot the ball out of the air in left field during the previous game now stood with their weapons drawn and formed a small line of protection between Billy in left field and the spectators, their eyes roaming the entire crowd. They would remain in place for the rest of the game.

"It's the bottom of their order," called Long John Dillon, slapping his mitt. "Set 'em down, Dix, and let's get back in there and end this thing."

Dixie mustered up all he had left, and to everyone's delight, he retired both Dalrymple and Flint, the first two batters, easy as swatting flies—or catching one fly and striking one out, as the case happened to be.

Retiring the third batter, Corcoran, however, proved to be a tougher task. Batting left-handed for the first time that day, the feisty little hurler swatted an inside pitch right over John Dillon's head for a single.

That brought up the Chicago leadoff man, McVey, who surprised everyone by setting down a bunt toward Tonio, who came charging in from third. Taking the only chance he had, Tonio barehanded the ball and rifled it to first, but his throw did not catch the fleet McVey.

Jack had sprinted into shallow right field to back up the play at first and spied Corcoran taking a wide turn at second.

"Two!" he blurted just as Uncle John was catching the throw. "Two!"

Uncle John responded with a bullet toss to Jésus, covering second, but Corcoran managed to scramble back safely on hands and knees.

Dixie looked spent. Cooling down during the rain spell, then warming up again had put a strain on the old soldier's wing. He was, however, their number one pitcher, and Jack knew that as long as he had the will, he would pitch.

When Joe Quest fouled off pitch after pitch, for what seemed like ten minutes, and finally earned himself a walk, Dixie took his time regrouping.

Jack realized that staring in from the pitcher's box and seeing the likes of King Kelly approaching, with bases loaded and the game on the line, could take the final muster out of even the most stouthearted man.

But Dixie's old heart was stouter than most. He glared into the Irishman's eyes, spat a stream of tobacco juice at him, then proceeded to fire a feisty pitch.

Kelly strode into it, like the skilled batsman he was, driving a liner out toward Billy in left field.

Yes, thought Jack. Out number three!

Billy read the sharp fly as best he could. He backed up, then scooted right, then realized the topspin on the ball was sinking it. He tried to recover from the misplay, dashing in as fast as he could, but slipped, and only managed to snag the ball after it had kissed the outfield grass.

Corcoran ran home with the go-ahead run.

And the bases were still loaded.

Jack winced at the effort, but what could he do? "Focus on it, Billy. You'll get 'er next time. Catching is just like hitting. Just gotta lock on."

Billy returned to his spot and began pawing the crabgrass with his feet. Jack grinned, for he knew what Billy was doing. He was searching for a sharp stone nearby to scuff his boots on.

Dixie took the blame, though, kicking the dirt and stomping and for the most part looking disgusted with himself. After knocking down the following hitter, George Gore, twice, Dixie finally cooled off and settled in at least enough to get the big man to swing and miss at two straight pitches. But on the next pitch, Gore made solid contact. He drove the ball deep over Billy's head in left field.

Oh, no, thought Jack, watching it sail away. That's it. A grand slam, four-run homer. Suddenly, he felt greatly sorry for Billy. Had he caught the line drive—one that even Buckles could've handled—had he not slipped, it never would've come to this.

But Billy *was* a fighter. Even with this tall blast, he was giving it his all.

Chasing after the deep drive, Billy ran straight into the crowd. There being no fence, the entire field was considered fair territory, and the crowd moved away quickly. But nobody moved the small three-tiered set of bleachers standing directly in Billy's path.

This, Jack decided, would be interesting.

Billy spotted the wooden planks just in the nick of time. And like a dancer, he jumped to the third row, then off the back, and hit the dirt beyond, still moving at a good clip. That brought a surprised cheer.

Turning his head once again to the sky, Billy did something very few men in the world could've done. He found the small white ball in all those clouds, and locked on. And just as it fell to earth, he raced under it, pulling his hands into his gut. He ran ten more steps before turning around and holding the baseball high for all to see.

Three outs. Amazing. Gunshots from his armed guards added to the ecstatic roar.

A great catch, sure, and the inning was over. But the White Stockings led, ten to nine.

"I ain't got much left," said Dixie as he took a seat on the dugout bench. "Boys, let's wrap 'er up."

Larry Corcoran, ten years younger than Dixie
Bodine, displayed nothing but vim and vigor as he took his place
in the pitcher's box for the bottom of the tenth. His whip and his
jump as he warmed up stirred a nervous flutter in Jack's stomach. Luckily, Billy was there.

"I'm supposed to bat right before you, son," he said, placing
his palm on Jack's shoulder. "Got any advice?"

"Well, sure I do," said Jack, snapping out of his gloom. "First
off, scratch up those slick shoes. Or did you already?"

Billy tilted his foot, showing deep crosshatches in the leather
sole.

Jack nodded, but could not even utter an "attaboy" before
they heard a sharp crack. Blackjack Buck had opened the inning
with a double to right center!

The crowd bellowed and stomped, rocking the grandstands.
Jack grabbed Billy and spun him around, hooting in glee. The
tying run was aboard!

"Just watch" was all he could say to Billy now. "Just watch."

Fence Post strolled up next and took a while to kick himself a
new hole in the moist dirt, which, by the time he was done, had

swallowed two inches of his height. But he looked well fortified and ready to lay into one.

On the third pitch, he did. A steaming line drive shot from his bat, right back at Corcoran, who ducked just in time as it headed for center field. However, second sacker Cal McVey had a different notion. Getting an astounding jump, he darted deep to his right and snagged the ball on the fly, robbing Fence Post of a sure hit and forcing Blackjack Buck back to second.

I never should've given him his glove back, thought Jack. But it was too late now.

While Rico Del Rey approached the plate, Jack escorted Billy, next in line, over to the on-deck area.

"Next thing you do, Billy, is you grab that iron bat lying there."

Billy bent down and retrieved the horseshoe bat Rico had just dropped and gave it an awkward swing.

"Heavier than I thought," he said. He tried it once more with a jerky motion that looked as if he were holding a rope with a bull yanking on the other end.

Jack sized up the situation, but after weighing all the factors, including the vital runner on second and the game being on the line, he finally leaned over and softly said, "Billy, what do you think about trying to bunt one? With your speed, I think it would be a sure thing."

Billy shook his head. "That's the type of thing you boys can pull off, but not me."

"Okay, okay." Jack puzzled on it a moment. Somehow, he

had to come up with a plan ensuring that Billy would not make an out. "Well, what about letting the ball hit you?"

"Do what?"

"It's a great plan, Billy. What if you sort of accidentally lean over a close one and let it tick your arm or something?" Jack demonstrated with a spin.

"Let it wing me?" He did not look happy about that.

"One strike on the batsman!" called Barnaby.

"Come on, Rico!" yelled Jack over Billy's shoulder. With the crowd roar and the calls from the rest of the team, Jack doubted Rico could hear a thing, but he shouted just the same. "Drive him to home."

The next pitch came low, and Jack again turned to Billy.

"Okay, never mind about getting hit by the pitch. Just use your chili-pepper skills and hit it where they ain't. Try your best. Do anything you can to get on. But if you *get* to first base, and second base is open, you have to use your speed to steal second."

"You act like I would know how to do that, too."

Jack slammed his hands to his hips, spun on one foot in a full circle, and landed right back in front of Billy, staring him in the eyes. "Okay, okay, here's how. All you do is run to second base when the pitcher pitches the ball."

"Just like that."

"Sure." He nodded toward Corcoran. "Watch him. As soon as he starts his run to pitch, you start your run to second. That's why it's called stealing."

Billy grinned. "Well, I have been known, in the past . . ."

"I know, but this kind of stealing is pure legal."

"Strike two on the batsman!"

The dugout was in an uproar, clapping, shouting out encouragement at the top of their lungs.

"Rico," called Jack. "Focus! Hit it someplace, anyplace, with all your might."

Billy was still waving the horseshoe bat, flinging it back and forth now like a wheat scythe.

"You know," he said, "I could've used a little more practice."

"I know. But it will have to do." Jack pointed. "While you're swinging that thing, watch Corcoran pitch and get your timing. That will help." He paused before adding the obvious, as casually as he could. "I'm up to bat right after you, brother. So you better do something big. Remember, I got me a broken hand."

Billy turned to watch Corcoran's next pitch. This time, he swung the heavy bat swiftly and in perfect timing with the pitch.

"That a way," said Jack. "That swing right there is what you want." He rubbed his hands together. "I'm starting to get a real good feeling about you now." The feeling, however, did not last all that long.

"Freeze right there, Billy Bonney!"

A huge voice cut through the crowd. From around the corner of the White Stockings dugout, Marshal Danbridge stepped out onto the field with his gun drawn. "You're wanted dead or alive. So it's your choice, Kid. Make it easy on yourself or easy on me." Danbridge aimed his weapon with both hands.

At that instant, Uncle John sprinted toward Danbridge. "No, you don't!" he yelled. "We let you take Shadowfox. We won't let you take this'un."

Using the distraction, Billy spun in a circle, still clutching the bat, dropping down and rolling toward the dugout.

Jack hit the dirt, too, as everyone in the line of fire ducked or scattered.

Danbridge leveled his gun at Billy, following him with the gun barrel as he rolled. And before Uncle John could reach him, as Billy rolled up to the lip of the dugout, Danbridge fired.

Bang!

Jack could only watch as Billy, still rolling, used the momentum of his spin to swing that iron bat—quicker than a bubble bursting.

And in that instant, *he hit the bullet.*

Smack dab, dead center, on one of those lucky horseshoes, Billy the Kid connected. The quickest hands in the land swatted that little piece of lead right back at the shooter.

The bullet flew on a sharp line and caught Marshal Danbridge in the middle of the forehead, knocking him flat on his back. He did not get up.

As the spectators began to realize what had just happened, they stood up in the stands in a stunned shroud of awe and amazement. By the time Doc Hathaway climbed down from his perch, Danbridge lay sprawled on the ground, lifeless.

"Looks like he's been clocked with a rock," said Doc. "He's a goner, all right. He's got no pulse."

"I told him he should've left town," said Long John Dillon.

"Take him away. And have some boys start digging a hole up on Last Out Hill."

He turned to Billy. "Son, that was the finest display of hitting these old eyes have ever seen."

And that was true for everyone. Not only had Billy saved his own life, but he had become the first man in the history of baseball to hit a bullet line drive.

Before the game resumed, Jack again sidled up to the outlaw, who was still gripping the lucky horseshoe bat.

"Tell me, son," said Jack. "Will that be enough batting practice for the time being?"

Billy did not bother answering. On the very next pitch, Rico struck out.

Billy's eyes carried a wagonload of concern as he started off for the home stone, coming to bat as he was with two outs and the game on the line.

Blackjack Buck, the tying run, was still standing on second, the crowd was still cheering, and Jack could do nothing but hope that one or two baseball angels were still around.

On the first pitch, an inside fastball, Billy leaned way over the stone, turning his back to it. The ball nearly hit his left arm as he pulled it back at the last instant.

He frowned at Jack, who waved his hands. "No, forget it."

The next time, Billy stood normally. Patiently. He choked up, just as Jack had taught him during chili pepper, and took a couple of practice swings.

He waited. On the next pitch, Billy banged a single to center field.

The place went *loco*. Gunshots, drumbeats, whoops, and whistles. The noise alone seemed to carry Blackjack Buck all the way home. Now the score was ten to ten, and the home team was still alive.

And, for the moment, the town was, too.

Jack closed his eyes with a strange mix of relief and consternation, and mumbled an even stranger mix of "Thanks" and "Thanks for *what*?" as he walked up. Finally, his true moment of glory had arrived, and he could not even hold the bat.

Glancing around, Jack saw Billy step off first base, taking a small lead.

Jack froze, turning to him, widening his eyes, trying to shout with them, trying to shout, "No! Don't go."

The man cannot possibly steal a base with such a tiny lead, he told himself. He'll be out, and I'll be to blame.

Not knowing whether Billy had read his signal or not, Jack stepped up to the stone. Through the pain, he held the bat as best he could, keeping half an eye on what Billy was doing.

Uncle John clapped his hands. "Hit it hard, son!"

Ah, thought Jack, if only I could.

Billy casually crouched and watched the pitcher, just as Jack had coached. So far, so good. The instant the pitcher ran forward, though, Billy darted off the base, heading for second.

There was only one thing Jack could think to do. He squared around, as if he were going to bunt the ball, but he didn't. He missed it on purpose, holding the bat directly in front of the catcher's eyes as long as possible, to help protect Billy as he ran.

Billy, however, stole the base easily, arriving well before the throw. Jack quickly turned toward Uncle John and nodded, as if to say, I told him to do that. Pretty good idea, right?

"Just do your job, son," Uncle John's big voice bellowed. "Hit it some place hard."

Jack nodded. *Hard?* Maybe he should lean into the ball like he'd told Billy to do. That would be about as hard as he could hit it.

The next pitch was high and outside, and to everyone's amusement, Billy again stole a base. Now he was on third.

Jack stared at him, hoping this time his eyes could speak louder than before and tell Billy *not* to steal home. With two outs, especially. It would be too dangerous.

Billy grinned.

Oh, no! Jack stepped back a moment, away from the stone, glaring with eyes that demanded—no, commanded—Billy, don't try it. *Don't steal home.*

However, with one hand on his hip, Billy made his other hand into an imaginary pistol and fired a shot at Jack. Everyone laughed.

"That's right," someone yelled. "Hit a bullet!"

But Jack knew Billy's sign did not mean that.

Squeeze, thought Jack. Billy was calling for the squeeze play they had talked about last night. Was he wacky?

Jack could see it. Billy would run home with the pitch, but the ball would get there first, and Billy would be a dead duck.

Didn't he remember what he'd told Jack last night about not thinking anything was for sure? Did Billy now think that stealing a base was so easy that they couldn't get him?

Jack stayed away from the stone a moment longer, searching for ideas. A RIM play? Sure, Jack could bunt the ball, but with two outs, he would have to make it to first base for Billy's run to count. That would take a perfect bunt. And he could not even grip the bat to guide it.

He shook his head at Billy. *No!*

Billy winked. What did that mean?

"Drive him home, boy!" yelled Fence Post. Uncle John paced and clapped. "Wait for your pitch, son. Wait for a good pitch."

Corcoran licked his fingers. Jack held the bat one-handed and tapped it on the ground. He strode forth and assumed the best stance he could. As the pitcher started his run, Billy did too.

Yep, thought Jack, he's coming.

"He's stealing home!" the shortstop yelled.

"Get him, Flint!"

"Tag him out!"

There was only one thing Jack could do. Recalling what Jésus had done earlier in the game, Jack decided it was his only chance. He slid his good hand up the bat handle. He watched the ball sparrow-hop on its way in, from belt high to knee high in a blink, and focused on the white blur as best he could.

Billy may have started off before the pitch was delivered, but he'd made it only halfway home by the time the pitch arrived.

Holding the bat like a hatchet, Jack tomahawked the ball. It bounced straight down, then straight up. He took off running.

He saw the pitcher dart in toward the first-base line, then stop, waiting for the ball to come down. He didn't wait long. As Jack breezed past, Corcoran leapt up to snag the ball out of the sky.

Jack bore down, focusing on the eyes of Cap Anson, trying to read in them the trajectory of the oncoming throw. If he could place his body between the ball and Anson's mitt, the throw would never arrive.

But all he read in Anson's eyes was panic. What throw? It never came.

Corcoran had bobbled it. Jack crossed the bag. And Billy crossed home. Safe all around. *The squeeze play worked!*

Cincinnati, here we come!" Dixie
Bodine hoisted his mug and everyone leaned over to clink their
steins with his.

"We showed 'em!" said Fence Post. "It took a bit of trickery,
thievery, and a dose of tomfoolery, but we won it, fair and
square."

The celebration went on for hours. It had started at the ball
field where the crowd had boosted Jack and Billy onto their
shoulders and carried them all the way to La Plaza de Oro, where
Tia Rosa hosted a magnificent feast. From there they marched
into every saloon in town, and had now, in the wee morning
hours, stumbled into the rock cave clubhouse.

"We are the best team in the land," yelled Fence Post, for the
hundredth time. He slumped against the bar, adding softly,
"The best. Root beer floats all around . . ."

It was almost dawn. As the energy in the room died down,
Jack could barely sit or stand. Presently, he became most concerned with finding a decent spot to catch some shut-eye. It had
been a long day at the end of a very long journey.

A few other men had the same notion.

Running out of spots and bedding, Jack finally relocated himself to the base of the dirt wall where his fresh pile of soft dirt awaited. Out of the way and a little darker, it seemed as good a spot as any to curl up and dream, dream, dream.

He stretched out. A fine bed. He rolled up his overshirt to use as a pillow.

But he would not sleep. At least, not yet. John Dillon seemed to have something on his mind. And from his place at the head of the royal table, he banged his empty mug and called for quiet.

Jack could not quite see him, but he could hear him loud and clear.

"Men," he began. "Do you know the saying that the best things in life are free?"

"Sounds familiar," said Fence Post. Several others agreed.

"Well," said Uncle John, "it doesn't mean what you might think. It doesn't mean the best things don't cost anything. Means that they—the very best things—are unencumbered, untrapped, unchained. They are free."

"I'll testify to that," said Billy.

"The very best thing in life," John Dillon continued, "is when you can go anywhere you want, and no one tells you what to do. And the worst thing is when you're under someone else's control. Nothing beats freedom, boys. Even money."

"Okay," said Tonio. "We buy that. So, what are you saying?"

"I'm saying I will not be going with you to Cincinnati. I like it right here. We proved our point. We beat 'em. Now, if you boys want to go, it's your right. And I wish you well. But I have decided I'd rather sell my team to you gentlemen and stay right here than travel back in time into a part of the country I want no part of anymore."

The silence was heavy.

"Facing Cap Anson on the field today," Uncle John went on, "brought it all back to me. I want no part of it a-tall."

"But what will you do, Cap'n?" asked Rico. "You'll have no team."

"I will build another team. Done it many times before. And I will live a full and free life of playing baseball and growing apple trees. We are four thousand feet in the sky. This is three-month-a-year apple country and nine-month-a-year baseball country. And God's country all year 'round."

It took Dixie Bodine to put a fine point on the matter. Slowly, he rose.

"I left the South," began the ace hurler, "not because I was bitter about our boys losing the war, though I confess I had been for the longest time. No, I left because one day I stood up in church and sang 'Amazing Grace' as if I had never sung it before. And I saw that I had been blinded by a certain belief about certain folks with skin color darker than mine. It was a belief I no longer held. So I, too, don't mind staying put. For I once was blind, but not no more. And after what my cap'n just said, now I see better than ever."

Well, you could have heard a grain of dirt drop from the wall.

In fact, as Jack lay there, he heard a whole clump drop, coming loose from the weakened wall and cascading onto his chest.

With a *plunk*. For it was not only dirt that came a-falling. On top of it all sat a shiny yellow nugget of gold.

Jack jumped up and began wiping his hand across the wall, dusting away more loose dirt and exposing a yellow vein encased in quartz at least a foot wide.

All that shooting, all that dirt dumping, had exposed another great vein of gold in the Lucky Strike Mine that no one had ever dreamed was there.

He turned. "Boys," he whispered, hoarse as a bullfrog, "I believe I'm going to stay put, too."

This the land you're talking about?" asked Jack.

Billy rose up in his saddle and surveyed the panoramic view in the early morning light atop Dog's Ridge.

"It's beautiful," he said. "Paulita, boy, she will love it."

He pointed. "I'm runnin' cattle down there. My house goes right here." Billy slapped his saddle. "And down the slope a ways, apple trees."

"Apple trees?"

"Well, you never know how this baseball business is all gonna work out."

Jack laughed. "That's for sure."

They stood their horses, still looking, avoiding the moment until it could be avoided no more.

"I wish you'd take me with you, Billy."

"Hey, now."

"I know, but—"

"But, nothing. You take the money, like we said. Buy this quarter section from your uncle John before the price goes up. Three hundred twenty acres. And I'll be back. But while I'm gone, I need a good man to watch over things for me."

"This whole town will watch over you, Billy."

"I do get that sense."

Jack took a hard swallow as the silence and the vast pine mountain scenery enveloped them both.

Finally, Billy slapped Jack's arm with his hat. "Don't take no wooden nickels, son."

Billy backed his horse away from the ridge crest. "And don't take no more sass talk from Jésus. Respect, my foot. You won her over fair and square."

That forced Jack to flash a quick glance at Billy, grin, and look away.

"You heard what I said." Billy tisked his horse, turning. *"Adios, amigo."*

John Jefferson Jackson Dillon could not bring himself to say good-bye. He was all of a sudden throat-swoggled. But he watched, as best he could, through the blurry mist that had somehow blown up and filled his eyes.

He took a deep breath, watching Billy gallop away. Into the sunrise. Into a new day.

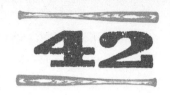

Later on down the line . . .

Billy never did make it back to Dillontown. One evening, around midnight, a couple of months later, Billy rode to Pedro Maxwell's *hacienda* outside Fort Sumner, New Mexico, to visit with Paulita.

Lying in ambush were three lawmen, Lincoln County Sheriff Pat Garrett and two of his deputies. As Billy entered Pedro's room to ask about two of the strangers he'd spotted outside, he had no way of knowing Pat Garrett was in the darkened room as well.

The Kid was unarmed. Garrett fired away. On that night, July 14, 1881, Billy Bonney died. Pat Garrett received a combined total of $2,500 in reward money from businessmen and the government, which he used to buy a little ranch in New Mexico.

William Hulbert, a desperado businessman in the eyes of many, did not last long either. A few months later, at age forty-nine, Hulbert died of a heart attack in Chicago. But before he died, he had managed, in cahoots with Cap Anson and A. G. Spalding, to steal the game of baseball from a multitude of ballplayers. The ban on African-Americans in major-league baseball denied millions of men, women, and children the joy of baseball at its finest. And the effects are still being felt today.

Beyond that, as Blackjack Buck had dreamed, Hulbert's infamous Reserve Clause, which the National League president had initiated in 1875, continued to haunt baseball players for nearly a century, until—as his prophecy put it—the hundred-year flood washed it away. That is, Curt Flood, an African-American ballplayer from St. Louis, Missouri, started litigation that eventually led baseball to amend the clause in 1975.

In 1885, four years after our story ends, Long John Dillon retired as a player and became the team's full-time manager. In the early 1900s, with the help of a German immigrant, Dr. Karl Altenheimer, Cap'n Dillon finally completed the ballpark of his dreams in a dry lake bed near the Lucky Strike Mine. Though it has seen both good times and bad, the Lucky Strike Park still stands today.

In 1888, on the day before his marriage to Eliza, Jack officially adopted a surname honoring his parents and their ancestral town of La Croix. And to honor Eliza's heritage, they agreed to use the Spanish version of the name, which is La Cruz.

Their five children all carried the name de la Cruz.

They all lived their lives in Dillontown, too, except for Jack and Eliza's oldest son, Billy Henrico, who claimed the town was getting too big. In 1915, Billy Henrico de la Cruz moved his young family about fifty miles east, to the little village of Paloma.

But, my friends, that's another story.

Author's Note

Fair Warning:

No interior, exterior, nor ulterior motive is to be found or implied within the preceding text. Anyone caught searching for some such will be mortified by the effort.

Having said that, the careful reader may yet stumble upon certain historical facts around which this folderol has been concocted. For instance: The wealthy coal mine operator, Mr. William Hulbert, did in fact own the 1880 National Champs, the Chicago White Stockings, whose entire roster has been correctly identified in this book along with various personal foibles. Beyond that, baseball's repugnant Reserve Clause and its despicable sixty-three-year ban on hiring African-American ballplayers can be traced to Hulbert and his Chicago organization as well. And yes, there were seven balls to a walk that year (six balls, the next), and the pitcher did pitch from only 45 feet away. As speed increased, so did the pitching distance, along with the use of catchers' mitts and such.

References to the life and times and Billy the Kid, including his desire to quit outlawing and his affection for

Paulita Maxwell, are based on sound historical research. His trip out West, as depicted herein, was, however, pure concoction, sparked solely by the fact that Billy's precise whereabouts after his final jailbreak on April 28, 1881, were at times rather unknown.

I thank you kindly.

THE AUTHOR